BETWEEN THE LINES

The Book Beyond Time

James Pindras

Library of Congress Control Number:2019917171

Crown Images and Lion Image:
Courtesy of Omalepics: https://www.freepik.com/free-photos-vectors/vintage
Courtesy of Omalepics: https://www.freepik.com/free-photos-vectors/banner
Courtesy of Dreamstime: ID 8506365 © Mirumur | Dreamstime.com

Printed in the United States of America

First Printing: Nov 2019

ISBN-13 978-0-5785949-8-9

Library of Congress Control Number: 2019917171

My deep appreciation and heartfelt thanks To Amanda Redgrave, for the enormous contribution you made to the completion of this book, in time, character development as the inspiration for Lady Amanda, for your edit suggestions, and in reading and rereading manuscript drafts Lastly, thank you for believing in me and trusting me to tell this story. Thank you for believing in me and trusting me to tell your story.

My Thanks To Steve Ruegg for his time as a Beta Reader and editing suggestions.

My thanks To C.J. Anya for her professional editing services.

Table of Contents

GLOSSARY

Ignominia – Latin - dishonorable/disgraceful

The Noble Houses of Aquitaine
House of the Lion – Lord Leo/Lord Jacques/Lady Amanda
House of the Osprey – Lord Phillip
House of the Wolf – Lord Alexandere
House of the Lynx – Lord Stephan
House of the Badger – Lord Robert

Steadfast Houses
House of the Bear – Lord Bernard
House of the Fox – Lord Chevell
House of the Panther – Lord Henri
House of the Eagle – Lord Lucian
House of the Mouflon – Lord Percival

To my family thank you for your love and support

AUTHOR'S NOTE

The following story is fantasy and is not an accurate history or description of Twelfth-Century Aquitaine. Some of the characters are based on historical figures, but the main characters and those of the ten Nobel Houses are fictitious. France, both past and present-day, and the city of Boudreaux are a backdrop for a magical journey. This journey will happen to you if you willingly enter into the endless possibilities of wonder and imagination. Enjoy your journey, and remember, "Readers have reported losing themselves within the pages of this book. Be careful, or your life will change in ways that are most extraordinary and unanticipated!"

"The end depends on the beginning."
- MANLIUS 1ST CENTURY ROMAN POET

PROLOGUE

Jake sat back in his favorite chair, covered by his wife's favorite, soft wool blanket. Looking back over the long years, he was grateful for the rich and varied life he had lived. As his eyes scanned his library, he focused on pictures of his wife, Manda, their children, and his granddaughter, thinking about how much he loved them. As he shifted his gaze to the shelves filled with a vast array of books, he smiled and said aloud, "No, my dear friends, I haven't forgotten how much you too, have changed my life."

Jake looked down at the book in his hand. At first glance, it wasn't much to look at. A tired, old book with a worn leather cover and faded gold lettering. He reread the title, The Boy Who Would Be King. The book felt warm and alive in his hand and looked like it was made in the 1800's. However, Jake knew it had no printing date on the cover page, it was ancient beyond counting, and many people throughout the ages had held it close to their chests the way he did now. Jake realized he was coming to the end of his life, and he took stock of the years, smiling as he remembered how wonder entered his life.

CHAPTER ONE

Jake wolfed down his dinner, barely pausing to breathe.

"Jake, why the rush?" his mother asked.

He started to explain talking around the food stuffed in his mouth, but his dad laughingly said, "Please, Jake, finish that mouthful before telling us."

Once Jake finally swallowed the last bit of food and washed it down with some milk, he told his parents that today, he'd been given the first book of his very own from his Uncle Jerry. He described how he carefully unwrapped the gift paper as his uncle had told him the book was his favorite, coming from his own library collection.

His uncle said, "Jakey, I have loved this book for many years, and I think you, too, will find it both strange and wonderful. I want it to become the start of your library."

Jake had hugged his uncle, saying, "Oh, thank you! I'll always treasure it."

After he finished eating, and promised not to stay up too late reading, Jake ran up to his room and turned on the lights. He glanced at his walls filled with his hand-drawn pictures of what he imagined some of his favorite characters looked like. He felt the well-worn, and slightly scuffed leather, cover between his fingers. He could tell its age by the yellowed pages and the slightly bent corners. There were flourishes on the leather cover and worn gold guilt used to print the title of the book The Boy Who Would be King. He didn't remember ever seeing it at his uncle's house before. Then again, there were so many books in Uncle Jerry's library that Jake surely would have missed a few.

Lifting the book to his nose, he drank in the smell of old paper, and ink. It was a magic elixir that always drew him in. When he opened the thick cover, he thought he smelled a hint of… perfume? As he held the book, it seemed to swell as if taking in a deep breath, stretching after being closed for ages and coming alive again like his mom's tulips in spring. He smiled at the thought and ran his finger gently up the book's spine and the gold-gilded edge of the pages. Jake felt the book tremble in his hands. Surely it must have been his fingers shaking because he was so excited about his first, book.

As Jake opened to the cover page, he noticed the pages felt less brittle than before. Looking down, he saw a drawing of a boy in very fine clothes. Jake supposed the boy in the picture was the same boy from the title. The boy had handsome features and dark, unruly hair, his expression stern. He thought, the boy seemed a little full of himself, but then thought, I would be a little full of myself if I were to become King. Turning to the first page, he read:

Dear Reader, you are about to embark upon a most strange and a wonderful journey. This book is filled with stories of good and
evil and love and war, but beware! Readers have reported losing
themselves within the pages of this book. Be careful, for your life
will change in ways that are most extraordinary and unanticipated!

Jake thought the warning a little weird. It must have been some old-fashioned way to get people to read the book. Shrugging, he continued to the first chapter.

Chapter Two

Master Jacques

There was once a boy named Jacques who was of the Noble House of Lion and lived long ago in the faraway Kingdom of Aquitaine. He was tall for his age and a little clumsy, but he loved to ride his horse and explore the forests surrounding his family chateau that had been in the family for generations. The chateau was large and rambling, and on the front door, someone long ago carved a fierce-looking lion. The rooms were large, with many fireplaces and furnished with comfortable furniture. Many of the rugs and fabrics were in different shades of blue. On the walls were several portraits of his different ancestors, the Lords, and Ladies from long ago. Also, there were arrangements of different weapons and brightly painted shields telling the history of the House of Lion, from a different perspective.

There was also a large garden his mother loved to tend. One of Jacques's strongest memories was of the scent of the freshly cut blooms his mother arranged and placed around the house. The chateau had many rooms and nooks Jacques loved to investigate. The cellars, attic, and stables were some of his favorite places to inspect because there were always little treasures that were lost or secreted away and forgotten. Once he found an old broach his mother thought she'd lost forever. Another time,

Jacques brought an old, dried out scorpion to his mother, Amélie, as a birthday present. Hugging him, she laughed, saying, "Jaci, you will have to learn what a proper gift is for a lady!"

Jacques liked nothing better than telling silly jokes so he would hear his mother laugh and his father groan. Some thought him to be clever and intelligent for his age. Jacques never really thought about it. He just enjoyed attending the lessons of the tutors, his father Leo, had hired for him. Since he was of a noble line, it was not proper for him to attend a village school. Perhaps the one trait that best described Jacques was his insatiable curiosity. Had he been born in another time and another place, he would have been an explorer or scientist, but Jacques was happy with his life, his family and his friends.

Once, his father told Jacques he was born to a noble house that had fallen out of favor in the Royal Court. Father would never talk about the reason, only that it was a humiliation the family had to bear until one of their line performed an act of great courage. Jacques did not understand any of this.

Why, should they look down upon us because of what happened long ago? It is not fair! Soon after the conversation, Jacques reached his Name Day, the day they now considered him to be a man, and his world changed suddenly and unexpectedly.

The first and most devastating heartbreak happened when a plague struck the town. The people in the surrounding towns and villages became deathly sick with fever and boils, and many soon died. Leo's family was safe in their chateau, but Amélie would not allow herself to sit in safety, and watch people suffer and die. She accompanied the healers into the hardest-hit villages to relieve the pain of the sickest inhabitants. After some weeks, the worst was over, and the plague passed. Not long after, Amélie began to feel weak and feverish, taking to her bed. Leo called for the Healer Quintus to care for her.

Quintus soon discovered that after her tireless work helping the villagers, Amélie had exhausted herself and could no longer fight the disease. He did what he could, but it was soon clear it was not enough, and Amélie would soon join her Ancestors. Once, Jacques went to his mother's room to sit with her, but the healers and his father forbid it. He begged Leo to reconsider.

"I know if I could just hold her hand, she would get better! Please, Father, let me sit with her."

Leo said, "No, Jacques, and that is final! Your mother would not want you with her now. You could get sick too, and she would never forgive herself or me if something happened to you." Jacques, hurt by his father's cold tone and angry expression, ran off to cry in private. Jacques could not see or understand that his father already grieved the loss of his beloved wife. When Amélie passed, they gave her the full honors of a lady of a noble house and laid her to rest in the House of the Ancestors. People from far and wide came to the ceremony to pay their respects to Lady Amélie of the House of Lion. All agreed she was one of the kindest, most compassionate women they had ever known.

The second blow came to Jacques as he walked through the high-walled city of Bordeaux, Aquitaine's capital. As he approached his friends, most ignored him, and the others made cruel jokes about his name and House. Jacques could not understand why his friends were now his enemies. He was still the same person, and yet, all at once, Jacques was invisible. He became a nonperson unnoticed unless his former friends deigned to mock or ridicule him. They called him names like "low born" or "yellow mane" or "Minou" (French for kitty). The other names were vulgar, making him blush, causing him to run home in shame and embarrassment. Whenever Jacques ran home, his father would scold him, ordering him not to run away.

Leo said, "Son, you were born under an auspicious sign. You are destined for greatness. If you are to fulfill your destiny, you must stand your ground, especially in front of the other Houses. One day, you will command their respect and be honored by them. You are a man now, Jacques! This running ends now!! Do I make myself clear?"

You may ask yourself, why did his friends turn on him? Now that the adults considered the children to be of age, their fathers told them stories about the cowardly House of Lion; and of a shameful event that happened long ago. None of their fathers remembered the specifics of the story because they did not know how to read, and even if they had, they wouldn't have known where to look for the answers. None of that mattered now, because the young men of the other Houses knew Jacques by sight, and they never let him forget his shame or his place at the bottom of the pecking order. Nor would any of the adults of the other Houses, let the House of Lion forget their shame, remembering what an ancient and regal line the Lions were. They were the fiercest warriors in the long history of the Kingdom. The other Houses agreed that they should never allow the Lions to regain prominence because it would risk their positions of power.

After one especially brutal encounter, Jacques stalked home fuming, facing the same lecture from his father.

He mumbled, "Yes, sir." Looking for a distraction, he picked up a book from a table in the library and headed to his special quiet place to read and think. Jacques did what he always did when he was alone (which happened often). He read. It did not matter what he studied. He soaked the words on a page the way a sponge soaks up water. Jacques had never seen a sponge, but he had read that somewhere.

He walked through the winding streets and out the city gates until he found his favorite reading spot by the river, one flowing from the ancient forest. Perching on a worn boulder he started reading about Charlemagne the Great, a warrior king who unified the other kingdoms into a great power. Jacques learned that Charlemagne ushered in a new renaissance marked by an upsurge in art, literature, music, philosophy, and schools of learning. Besides being well versed in the art of war, Charlemagne proved himself to be an exceptional and wise ruler. Jacques felt proud that Aquitaine was a member of that long-ago empire during that heroic time.

As he read, he came across the history of a famous battle marked by one near disaster. As he read, his face burned red with shame. He finally discovered the answer to the House of Lion's disgrace. His great, great, grandsire had been a commander of one of Charlemagne's armies. The Lions distinguished themselves by their fierceness in war and the ability to read a battlefield like a book. The House had an uncanny ability to know just where the enemy was weakest, where the enemy would attack next, and they always knew the best grounds for the battle to take place. After reading this, Jacques was confused, *If the Lions were such renowned fighters, why are we now treated like cowards and traitors?*

Soon, he read about a crucial time in the battle where the enemy used a hidden gap in the hills to attack Charlemagne's flank, forcing his grandsire to retreat. The Lions quickly regrouped and turned the tide of battle leading to a victory. However, the other Lords, jealous of the skill in the battle of the Lions, told the emperor half-truths of vents during the battle. Later, Charlemagne questioned the loyalty and bravery of the House of Lion. When he discovered the truth, the Emperor reversed himself, but the damage was done, and the reputation of the Lions was tainted.

Jacques seethed with a fifteen-year-old's rage. "The injustice! The betrayal. The Lions were not cowards; the other Houses were by telling this lie repeatedly! Wait until father hears this! We will make sure the House of Lion is reborn!" Stomping up and down the riverbank, he waved his arms and yelled to the trees about this injustice.

However, the day was warm, and his anger had soon burnt out Jacques laid back on the rock and napped. He awoke when he heard a girl of one of the other Houses walking by. She was about his age with a collection of animals following her, seemingly rapt by the story she told. He saw a dog, a cat, a weasel, chipmunks, rabbits, squirrels, and a pig of all things. Jacques looked from the animals to her and immediately became enthralled. Not only was she the prettiest girl he had ever seen, but it was obvious both she and the animals understood each other. She didn't notice him until the dog barked, pointing out to her it was rude not to say hello.

She turned to the dog, saying, "Quite right, Rex; that was rude. Thank you for reminding me." Rex sat with his tail thumping against the ground, and the cat looked with disdain at such an undignified display and turned to lick his paw. The girl turned to face Jacques saying, "Hello there, it's about time you woke up sleepyhead. I am Lady Amanda of the House of Osprey. I don't believe we have met."

Chapter Three

Lady Amanda

*J*acques's mouth was as dry as the stone he sat on. His mouth moved, but no words came out. His mind was blank, and he could think of nothing to say. She was tall, and her long dark brown hair tumbled around her face and onto her shoulders. As he looked closer, it was her eyes that captivated him! Her eyes were a shade of green he'd never seen before, and after gazing into those eyes, he saw there was much more to Lady Amanda than any of the other young ladies he knew.

"Well?" said Lady Amanda, "can't you talk? Don't you know it is rude not to return a proper greeting? Even my dog knows that!" Rex gave the cat a smug look, and the cat looked disinterested.

Jacques swallowed and barely croaked out, "Hello, I am Master Jacques of the House of Lion. I am honored to meet you."

"That's better, for a moment I thought you were the village simpleton," said Amanda. She didn't intend for that to be as rude as it sounded. She lived alone with her father, who raised her always to be truthful. Without a mother's guidance, she did that in the most direct way possible. Besides, she hardly associated with the children of the other Houses, so she didn't understand how to talk to young people her age. She told herself it was because they were silly, but in truth she was shy. Besides the village children were a little afraid of her ability to have a conversation with any animal she saw. Lady Amanda thought it strange they could not. All one had to do was listen!

"It is nice to meet you too, Master Jacques. My, your name is quite a mouthful. From now on, I will call you, Jacques."

He didn't know what to think of that, but it was better than the other nicknames he had, so he just nodded. She looked closely into his eyes and said, "You don't say much, do you, Jacques? Are you sure you are not a simpleton?"

That snapped him out of his self-made enchantment. He didn't enjoy being called a simpleton once, much less twice in one conversation. Jacques stood up tall to his full height and said, "No! I am not a simpleton," flustered, thinking, maybe around this girl, he was one. "However, since you will call me Jacques, I will call you Amanda."

She smiled and said, "I would like that."

Jacques said, "I come out here often to read. How is it we have never met before?"

Amanda answered, "For the last two years since my mother died, I've been away at school, attending a convent in Mont-de-Marsan, but all they wanted to teach me was how to embroider on cloth and play music."

Jacques thought those were fine things to know but kept quiet. This girl intimidated him more than a bit. "You asked to come home?" Jacques asked.

"No!" Amanda said, laughing. "I just left. My father was not surprised to see me either." In the distance, she heard a bell ringing. "That is my signal to come home. It was nice to meet you. Maybe we will meet again along this path. Until then, Jacques." She walked back towards the sound of the bell, with her menagerie in tow.

Jacques stood there with his mouth hanging open, watching her walk away. He thought to himself, *I do not know what to make of this Amanda, but I hope I figure it out. She is unlike anyone I've met!*

Amanda was also flustered. She had never met a boy who read books! *I guess he is not bad looking, as boys go. Certainly not handsome, well, not yet anyway,* she said to herself. Amanda took one last look over her shoulder and chuckled, *and that hair! It looks like rabbits have nested in there!*

Although she admitted to herself, she sensed a wit and intelligence in him, and she liked his kind eyes. When meeting others, Amanda had a way of knowing things about them. She saw colors surrounding people she met, telling her the kind of person they were. Her father found this ability useful but warned her never to mention it. Most people did not understand such things. Amanda could also tell if people were trustworthy or not. Apart from her father, she could sense that Jacques was one of the most trustworthy people she had ever met. Amanda determined she would return to this path.

Lady Amanda dismissed her animals before walking into the front gate of her family chateau. It was a grand place with lots of windows, allowing the sun to shine in. It had marble floors with thick rugs in shades of yellow and green. It also held beautiful furniture. There was an amazing library filled with shelves of books covering nearly every subject. Amanda had secreted away a nice selection of books in her bedroom for moments when she wanted to be alone. Unfortunately, she didn't get much alone time as she had many duties around the chateau.

Amanda tried to sneak up the stairs to her room, but one servant saw her and told her that father's orders were to wash, change into fresh clothes, and join him in the ballroom straight away. After her mother, Lady Rachel, had passed, she was now the woman of the house. It was her responsibility to help entertain their guests. She hated entertaining! Mother made it look so effortless always knowing the witty things to say, ensuring the guests had full glasses and full stomachs. While she much preferred smaller gatherings of four or five close friends, her father always invited all the families from the nearby Noble Houses, like today. However, she knew better than to argue with her father and washed and changed.

As she walked down the grand staircase to the ballroom, she looked out over the sea of people, seeing a dizzying array of colors. She could always tell the boys her age from a distance. Their colors were mostly weak and ugly, causing her to cringe inwardly when they approached her to praise her for her beauty and talents. The worst offender was an older boy named Lucian from the House of Eagle who had a ridiculously high opinion of himself. Normally, she liked compliments, but these boys were not honorable; flattered her to get something from her. Not like the boy she'd just met. She sensed he was polite, sincere, funny, and honest. However, she also sensed he was broken in a way that she didn't yet understand, and she intuitively knew Jacques had a burning desire to right a wrong done to his House. She wondered if that was why he hadn't attended the party. Knowing her father was waiting, Amanda put Jacques from her mind so she could focus on her guests.

"Good evening, sirs," she said as pleasantly as she could. A chorus of "Hello, Lady!" was shouted back at her, setting her teeth on edge. They jostled each other to be in front, all speaking at once.

"Lady Amanda, promise me the first dance!"

"Have I told you how beautiful you are tonight?"

"That is a wonderful dress!"

So it went on and on. To change the subject, Lady Amanda said, "Tell me, do any of you know a boy named Jacques? Can you tell me what kind of boy he is?" She was shocked at the scornful laughter.

"Jacques, the Yellow Mane?"

"The minou from a litter of cowards?"

They all patted themselves on the back for their clever insults. She frowned; That didn't seem like the boy I met. They must be talking about someone else.

"I think you are mistaken. His name is Jacques. He is tall with dark unruly hair and a serious look," Amanda said. They laughed even harder.

"Amanda likes the fainthearted lion! Hahahahaha."

"Maybe they'll get married and have a pride of yellow lions."

"Hahahaha."

Amanda was not at all happy about their rudeness, especially because she had not yet made up her mind concerning Jacques. He seemed nice, not like this herd of swine. With her innate sense of fairness violated, Amanda stepped forward, breathing heavily green eyes blazing.

"Take care, boys," she said in a low, commanding voice. "You do not understand what you are talking about!" With that, the laughter stopped, as if someone flipped a switch. Together, the group took an involuntary step backwards, tripping over each other, and fell into a tangled heap. With that, she walked right on by and right into the ballroom looking for her father.

Her father had seen and heard everything. Phillip thought, *I will have to talk with Amanda about how the Lady of the House converses with her guests, no matter how rude they are. Though I wonder, could she really be interested in the young Lion? That will require more thought later.*

Phillip had nothing against the House of Lion. He respected the father, Leo, and wished he would accept his invitations to his parties. Besides, he always enjoyed his brief talks with Jacques, who seemed to be a fine young man, intelligent, and polite. Jacques impressed Phillip as the best-read boy in all of Bordeaux.

However, can Amanda be serious about him? She called him by such an informal and personal name. Still, she's always had a way of knowing what is at the heart of an individual and is seldom wrong. With that, Phillip put it out of his mind until later, greeting another guest.

After the party, the boys told exaggerated tales about what happened. Soon, wild stories sprang up all over town, like sparks from a wildfire.

"Did you hear that Phillip's daughter is engaged to the young coward?"

"Yes, and I heard she is a witch who controls animals and can kill with a look from those odd green eyes. No wonder the convent kicked her out!"

"I heard she has gypsy blood in her."

"How did she know my oldest daughter was with child again? Clara didn't even know for sure herself yet!"

"Phillip should take her to the priest."

There were other slanders the city gossips spread, all unkind and untrue.

Amanda couldn't have cared less about the gossips. "Let them choke on their lies," she said to Phillip when he told her about the stories.

Typical, he thought with a chuckle. Since her mother passed, she has become more headstrong. *No, that's not right, she has had to grow up too fast to take her mother's place as the Lady of the House. Besides my beloved Rachel had the same strength and character as Amanda.*

He closed his eyes, thinking on how much he missed his Rachel. He made his mind up to ignore the stories. *It is not a bad thing for a young woman to know her mind. I could not have done better than to have a wife and a daughter such as these. Amanda's intelligence and independent spirit will ensure she will not be taken advantage of or dominated by anyone. I hope whatever man she chooses will appreciate her and be worthy of her.*

In a time when such things were discouraged, Amanda grew up with the freedom to read, think, and have her own opinions, helping to shape her into the remarkable woman she was destined to become.

Jake stretched and looked at the clock on his nightstand. He rubbed his eyes.

Is that right? Midnight??

He quietly changed into his pajamas, brushed his teeth, and crawled into bed. Jake couldn't believe he'd read so far past his bedtime. He put the book on his desk and quickly fell asleep. That night, he had fantastic dreams.

The next day, Jake found it hard to concentrate on much of anything other than the book. When he was in class, he wondered what would happen next. Would Jacques redeem the honor of the House of Lion? What other strange and wonderful abilities did Lady Amanda have? He tried to picture Lady Amanda in his mind, trying to see her in the girls he knew. When Jake was at home, his mother often noticed a distant look in his eyes as he did his chores or at in front of the TV, and he had taken to wolfing down his meals so he could spend his precious alone time with Jacques and the Lady Amanda.

Chapter Four

Growing

Over the next few months, Jacques and Amanda spent more and more time together. They walked the fields (often with her animals) sharing stories of their lives before they met. As Amanda grew to know Jacques, she began to trust him more, and she described and demonstrated the abilities she had. Amanda understood animal speech, sensed the character and motivations of people she met, saw the auras surrounding them, and assessed the kind of person they were. She also had an awareness of those who had passed on and who remained near to those people they loved. Once, Amanda told Jacques how his mother visited him at night and sat by him, stroking his hair as he slept.

"She wants me to tell you, 'I know you miss me, Jaci, but I am by your side always. I have and always will love you. I cannot wait to see the person you are destined to be, my son.'"

Jacques immediately knew Amanda told the truth because no one but his mother called him Jaci. Then he turned away for a moment, squeezing his eyes shut so he wouldn't cry. Soon, he smelled the flowers his mother always loved, and he felt her warm embrace. With tears openly running down his cheeks, he smiled and thanked Amanda.

It amazed Jacques she could do such things. However, what impressed him most was her intelligence and her honesty. He grew to value her opinion on different subjects, even when those opinions differed from his. They had some heated conversations sometimes, and afterward, they'd agree to disagree but secretly believed themselves to be right. Truthfully though, as much as they hated to admit it, Amanda and Jacques shared many more interests and opinions than not. As she spent more time with him, Amanda began to understand she cared greatly about what Jacques thought of her.

Over the next several months, Jacques and Amanda spent hours together, talking, laughing, and sharing more about their lives, their hopes and dreams. He told her of his life and his love for books. Jacques spoke of riding his horse far afield to find some peace from all the commotion at the chateaux. He was unlike any of the other boys his age. He was curious about the world around him, and he loved to learn new things. Jacques told her how much he enjoyed the sessions with the tutors Leo hired, educating his son in philosophy, literature, and science. Also, by training in the art of war by a respected Man at Arms, Jacques could shed the embarrassment he felt from the constant taunting thrown his way by the other boys.

They both talked about the loss of their mothers and the holes it left in their young lives. Amanda told him what life was like as a woman in Aquitaine, something he honestly had never given much thought. She discussed the different responsibilities she held as Lady of the House. Amanda was to manage the household accounts, plan all the meals, plan and host her father's parties, shop at the market, supervise the household staff, and accomplish a host of other duties. Jacques had to admit Amanda was responsible for much more than he, and he agreed it to be unfair.

Amanda admitted while she would have preferred more free time, the practice she dreaded most was being courted by the young men of the other Houses. It was a long-held tradition intended to arrange suitable marriages between the different noble families. She told Jacques how most of the young Nobles made her cringe. Some were impolite while others were sloppy and smelled like a dirty horse stall. There were also arrogant ones who treated her like an ignorant girl whom they only wanted for her beauty and the influence of her House. Truthfully, Jacques had not thought of anyone else courting Amanda, and he especially could not imagine growing older without Amanda at his side.

As she spoke, he sensed her deep desire to have a more formal education in the arts and sciences and maybe even in martial arts. She told him of when she was a young girl and sat on the stairs, eavesdropping to visitors tell her father news of the world outside Aquitaine. Their stories only served to deepen her desire to know more.

Jacques understood and appreciated her frustration and hunger for knowledge. He began to share his lessons with her. He was not surprised at how quickly she picked up knowledge, even the most difficult concepts he barely understood, and she could discuss those ideas intelligently. Sometimes, when he told her of concepts, he did not fully grasp, Amanda could explain them to him in a different way so he understood. As she grew more important to him, Jacques promised himself if he could, he would find a way to make a formal education possible for Amanda.

When Jacques was alone, he often thought about Amanda. He remembered things he wanted to talk about with her later, writing little poems about her he never dared to share with her. Although, Amanda found two of his early poems in his messy handwriting, tucked away in a book he loaned to her. She debated whether to read them because she didn't want to embarrass him. However, her curiosity won out as she read:

> *Amanda, soon after we met*
> *I gave you my heart.*
> *Only to you with it*
> *would I so willingly part.*
> *For I know with you*
> *my heart is safe,*
> *As you hold it close*
> *in your warm embrace.*

A second poem read:

> *Amanda is…*
> *Light and dark.*

Fire and ice.
Laughter and sorrow.
Truth and contradictions.
Courageous and shy.
Strong and fragile.
More than beauty.
Wise beyond her years.
A free and untamed spirit.
I would not want her to be any other way.

Not very good perhaps, but to Amanda, who never had anyone write a poem about her, they were more beautiful than the poem about Tristan and Isolde by Béroul.

Sometimes at night, while trying to sleep, Jacques considered her ideas. Over time, he noticed he began to accept and appreciate many of her views, allowing his opinions to evolve just as hers did after hearing his ideas. When one would change their opinion because of something said, the other would sometimes tease them about being wrong but never in a mean way.

Jacques now understood that for the first time in his life, he completely trusted someone. He freely told Amanda everything about his life, including his House's reputation and how he'd discovered it wasn't true. He held nothing back from her as he realized that Amanda had broken through the shell he had built to guard himself against the cruel comments and taunts of the other children. It was only after Jacques took an honest look at his life that he realized how lonely he had been before he met her. Leo also noticed changes in his son, including a genuine smile every so often.

It's about time that he is enjoying life some, he thought.

During their walks over the fields and in the forest, Jacques and Amanda talked about what they knew concerning the different plants, their names, and their healing properties. Amanda was especially knowledgeable about the plants and animals of the forest. She knew them all by name, what they ate, and they told her things about the loud and clumsy humans. Amanda also shared stories of other strange creatures who lived deeper in the forest. These stories fascinated Jacques and he couldn't wait to meet these Woodland Folk. Also, with Amanda's instruction, he finally learned to understand the speech of some animals of the forest and even talked to them a little.

Amanda and Jacques were both growing, not only in stature or wisdom but also growing closer in spirit and respect for one another.

Time passed. Amanda kept taking Jacques deeper and deeper into the forest surrounding Bordeaux. Growing up, Jacques had spent a lot of time exploring the woodlands, but Amanda had discovered new and secret places he had never seen. In the spring, there were large clearings filled with nothing but daisies so white, it looked like it had just snowed. Jacques and Amanda would sit among the flowers and weave crowns of daisies for each other to wear, dissolving into laughter as they talked to each other using lofty language in regal voices. They would each pick a small tree branch and hold them like royal scepters. In the summer, they came across hillsides blanketed with red and orange poppies in colors so bright it hurt their eyes. They found other fields choked with wild roses in varying shades of white, pink, and red. As the summer waned, they walked through fields of lavender, breathing in the scent. In the autumn, they sat on a hillside and look over hundreds of tall sunflowers that covered every bit of open field and watched the birds and squirrels gather the seeds for winter.

Many times, they would walk into a certain clearing, and the hair would stand upon the back of Jacques's neck. He sensed that something ancient and elemental lived there though he seldom felt afraid because, whatever it was, it did not feel evil. Yet, it did not feel good either. It seemed as if it was above such "human" concepts. It was mostly unconcerned about what they thought and barely noticed their passing. Later Amanda told him what he felt was the Guardian of the Forest who is a being older than anyone could remember. It was indifferent to humans unless it concerned its domain and the welfare of its citizens. Amanda said she had heard stories from her forest friends that the Guardian would be capable of fierce wrath and appalling violence to those who violated the land or mistreated those under his protection.

Sometimes Amanda would take him to other clearings where the branches wove a canopy that covered them from the sun. The first time Jacques entered one, he knew it was a spiritual place. As the sun shone through the trees, it cast a green glow on everything it touched, including the two of them. Jacques would look about and marvel at how in those places were as green as the forest. Amanda would speak in hushed and reverent tones if she spoke at all. She was often silent in the deep woods, every so often motioning with a hand gesture for them to stop. Then Amanda signaled to him not speak and point to her ears. She would then close her eyes and smile as if listening to a symphony.

It was a long time before Jacques first started hearing what she did. Initially, it was soft, nearly inaudible. As Jacques listened more closely, he heard music within the forest. The wind rustled in the leaves, and the insects scurried about, talking to each other through clicks and whistles harmonizing with the leaves. He heard the deeper, louder sounds of the animals with their footsteps, snarls, and growls. Jacques heard the yips of laughter as one would share a joke to the rest of the pack. It was when the birds joined in with their songs that everything came together in a divine chorus. There were times he lost himself to the music, and when he came back to himself, he joyfully cried for the beauty of it all.

Much later, Jacques discovered the woodland music was created from the wind and the natural sounds of the forest, accompanied by the music of the Guardian, coming from deep inside the earth itself. In those times, the Guardian, moved by the great beauty of the forest, or sensing a need to send out a healing, sang out in love, playing the different bedrock formations like a human plays the piano. As he did so, all the Woodland Folk could feel the ground vibrate as did the trees of all shapes and sizes. When the Guardian sang, the trees would sway, and dance each in their own way. The movement caused their leaves to shiver in accompaniment. The singing also caused the boulders to rub against each other, adding a low bass rumble to the music. When violent thunderstorms gathered over the forest, the Guardian sang loudly to match the deafening thunderclaps. During spring showers, the song was soft, matching the patter of the raindrops. In the winter, the Guardian caused the branches to rub gently against one another, adding to the song of the snow softly falling.

Early in their wanderings, animals burst out of the forest and charged right up to Amanda. At first, Jacques stood before her to protect her. The animals would stop short and gave him an annoyed look. Amanda explained to Jacques they were friends of hers wishing to say hello. Soon, he got used to this and joined in greeting their friends. Jacques realized that Amanda was safe in the forest because the animals knew and loved her. She differed from other humans who came with their sharp sticks to hunt them or take their food of nuts, berries, mushrooms, and acorns back to the stone city.

After all the years of exploring the Ancient Forest, the number of different animals and creatures he'd never known, lived or even existed in there, surprised him. Amanda introduced him to unicorns (who are not as nice as you have heard). He met big, hairy man-like creatures who took turns dancing with Amanda. It delighted Jacques to meet creatures who looked like tiny voles. They were called Grand Surpis who, when threatened, grew to an enormous size. Amanda formally presented Jacques to the King of the Manticores, Leonitus, using his full name of Master Jacques of the House of Lions. Jacques was awestruck by the winged lion as Leonitus shook his golden mane out.

"Jaaaacques," he growled. It was the best pronunciation he could make with a mouth full of sharp teeth. "Aaaamandaaa has told us much about you, aaand we aaare most haaappy to make your aaacquaaaintaaance." His voice rumbled from his chest like the sound of wagon wheels on cobblestones.

After a moment of staring at the King with his mouth hanging open, Jacques bowed formally, saying it honored him to meet Leonitus, Lord of the Manticores. This greeting pleased Leonitus greatly. He had seldom met such a polite and intelligent human and granted Jacques full access to the forest surrounding the stone city, personally guaranteeing his safety. However, Leonitus also sensed an unfulfilled destiny that both Jacques and the other Woodland Folk would someday play a part.

The changing seasons held even more discoveries for Jacques as different Woodland Folk only came out in certain seasons. In the winter, there were Ice Fairies who painted the forest with frost and ice much as a human would paint a canvas. In the autumn, he saw colorful autumn leaves gathered in piles that would swirl, coming together in human form. They called themselves Feuilles Colorees. Their voices sounded like the crinkles and crunch of dried leaves, and they were deathly afraid of fire, even the tiniest spark. However, they could scatter themselves in the face of an enemy, startling them long enough to disarm them. In the spring and summer, Fire Fairies either led lost travelers home at night, or took them deeper into the woods, depending on their mood.

Others called the Vignes would wrap their long, thick vines around legs causing people to trip and fall. The Vignes unexpectedly introduced themselves to Jacques when he was leaning against a tree, talking with Amanda. Slowly, several vines crept toward Jacques and wrapped themselves around his ankles. At a signal, they dropped a heavy branch behind Jacques. Startled, he jumped and tripped, causing him to fall face forward. As he lay in the dirt, Jacques heard tiny peals of laughter. Amanda covered her mouth so he wouldn't see her silently laughing. The scene of Jacques lying face down in the mud is a story retold at Vigne gatherings to this day. The Vignes have a strange sense of humor.

Some of the happiest moments the young couple spent together were in the Woodland Folk's company and in wandering among the ancient trees of the forest.

22

With Amanda's teaching, Jacques could name different trees in the dark, sometimes by the touch of the bark, other times by feeling the tree's distinct energy. By knowing this, he could tell what part of the forest he stood in, day or night. However, as with all things, the responsibilities of adulthood and the outside world intruded on the joy of their secret refuge.

Word had reached Louis, King of Aquitaine, that a band of disgraced army deserters and mercenaries suitably named the Ignominia were making raids on the borders of the kingdom. King Louis sent a royal decree to the lords of all the Houses, telling them to assemble their best fighters and young men to drive the renegades back. Jacques was proud to be chosen from the House of Lion and to put his skills to the test. His father told him they would leave at the next full moon so Jacques should polish and oil his armor, sharpen his sword, and prepare for battle. He was sad to leave Amanda, but he was excited to show his father and the rest of the Houses that the Lions had claws that were sharp as ever. Unknown to anyone other than Amanda, Leonitus had secretly instructed Jacques in a fighting style known only to the Manticores and Leonitus was proud that Jacques had learned so well.

It was after one such exceptionally tiring lesson that Jacques fell asleep in the sunlight on the grass. Amanda found him lying there and said a prayer that he would be safe while fighting the Ignominia. She had heard rumors they were ruthless, holding no regard for the accepted rules of war. While he slept, she gently kissed him on the forehead and shook his shoulder to wake him. As his eyes opened, she said, "It's about time you woke up, sleepyhead." He jumped up, looking at the position of the sun, and he knew it was time to go. "Thank you for waking me," he said. "I have to finish packing because we leave at first light tomorrow. We won't be gone long, and I will have exciting stories to tell you when I come home. I promise I'll write to you every day!" With that, Jacques ran off towards home thinking of nothing but glory and honor hoping to regain the reputation of his House.

Amanda stood as still as a statue, watching him until his tiny figure disappeared over the hill. Tears openly fell on the blouse she wore, Jacques's favorite. *He didn't even notice what I was wearing, and no kiss goodbye either,* she thought bitterly. As she thought about his claim of returning home soon, she said, "No, Jacques, you will be gone a long time with this horrible business. Everyone new to battle thinks it will end quickly, but rebellions are long and hard-fought, and many men will die. It will be up to the living to carry on after the fighting and dying are over."

Over the next few days, Jake finished the book for the first time of many. In his dreams, he became Jacques, going on adventures with the extraordinary Amanda. He understood the feelings Jacques had for her because he felt that way about some girls he knew. Over the next year, Jake would pick the book up again and again to reread certain chapters and sections. As he read over time, he found he used more than his imagination to envision the story. Jake began to see the events as they happened in real-time, and rather than read the conversations, he would hear the different character's voices. At those times, it seemed he was transported into the book and back in time to Aquitaine. There were also times he noticed slight differences in the story, *I don't remember that,* but he would shrug it off because the story got better every time he read it. It was almost as if the book grew with him. Once Jake mentioned this to the one person who would understand. Uncle Jerry smiled, nodded his head and said, "You know, it seemed that way to me too. It is a magical book, isn't it?"

Later that night, Jake turned to the section where Jacques returned from battle with the Ignominia…

Chapter Five

Homecoming

*A*manda was right. Jacques did not return home soon. Not that autumn. Not that winter. Not that spring or summer. Amanda received only a few letters from Jacques, and alone in her room, she took them out from the secret place where she kept her most precious things. Unfolding the letters as she had done many times before, she read.

Dearest Amanda,

I apologize for not writing sooner. We have been marching for days. Father has been tutoring me in what to expect when we reach the frontier. All we do is ride, make camp, eat, sleep and break camp, and ride. It is both exciting and boring. The other day, a Chickadee friend of ours landed on my shoulder and said hello. It was good to see a friendly face, even if it was on a bird! He told me you are spending much time in the forest. In my heart, I wish I were there with you. The call to muster has sounded; I must go. I think about you every night before falling asleep. I will write soon!
J.

Amanda,

We are on the eve of the first big battle. The Ignominia have been probing our lines, but we keep pushing them back. Both armies are now in battle formation and ready to fight. We will show them, Amanda!

We will break them in our first charge! No one can withstand the might of Aquitaine! I have to go. Give my regards to your father. I miss you!
J.

Amanda,
War is nothing like I thought it would be. It is brutal on one's body and soul. We are constantly fighting without rest, and we have lost so many men so quickly. The Ignominia did not break on the first charge, or the second, or the third. They did not break at all, but neither did we! The officers are telling the men to stand fast, for this will not be over soon.
J.

Amanda,
Today, we won a battle but lost so many men. The Healer's tents are overflowing. Our dead are being sent back to Bordeaux in wagons. The enemy keeps attacking, looking for weaknesses, and we do the same. It seems the attacks are endless. Yesterday, we found one such weakness and disrupted their rear and supply lines. We must finish this! I must sleep.
Regards,
J.

Amanda,
It is over. I am coming home.
J.

As Amanda reread those letters, she saw the sweet and gentle young man she knew was slowly becoming a hardened warrior. She noticed in the letters, he seldom spoke of the wonders he saw around him or how much he missed her. Instead, he wrote more of the battles, tactics, and of the friends he lost in combat.

I was right about that too, she said sadly to herself. *How many have to die or get hurt until they learn that love and respect for one another solve more problems than fighting?* She wondered if she would recognize Jacques when he came home or if he would recognize her. Since he'd left, Amanda had grown from a girl to a woman, tall, straight, strong, and had matured into a distinctively rare beauty. The young Nobles (those whose fathers arranged for them to avoid the battles) had taken notice of her, overwhelming her father with requests to court her. Phillip knew how she felt about those boys, but he didn't want to offend the other Houses, so he allowed Amanda to walk with her suitors cautioning them that the decision to court was hers alone.

The men were gone for a year-and-a-half before dispatches arrived telling of the quashed rebellion and stories of a brave young Lion who won praise for his battle skills and his single-handed defense of their wounded king lying on the battlefield. The messenger said that the young Lion stood over King Louis, striking down any of the enemies who approached. They said the knight adopted some new fighting style no one had ever seen before. Those who were there said he looked like a Lion of old as he fought the Ignominia back time and time again until they ran in fear of him.

All of Bordeaux quickly went to work to prepare a celebration for the conquering heroes. In the surrounding towns and villages, dressmakers made large silk banners welcoming the men home. The Royal Agents traveled all over France to purchase the best wine. Food poured into the capital city. Meats and cheeses of all kinds filled the storehouses as well as flour and eggs for bread and pastries that would cleanse the palate between courses. Hordes of chefs and their assistants flooded the city; the carpenters worked day and night to build the trestle tables and benches to seat their victorious warriors. As the army drew closer to Bordeaux, the workers in the city and villages continued day and night on the preparations for the victory celebration. All within the kingdom wanted everything to be perfect for when their men appeared on the road to Bordeaux.

It was a perfect day as the army appeared on the road over the horizon. The sky was a deep blue with hardly a cloud visible. New flags and banners flapped in the breeze as if the city itself was waving to welcome the army home. Tables were set up in the square in the city center and loaded with food and wine. Families and sweethearts dressed in their finest clothes displayed the coats of arms of their Houses. As the army entered the outskirts of the city, the citizens gathered along the road, loaded with baskets of yellow and red flower petals (the royal colors of Bordeaux). When the army processed through the streets of Bordeaux, loud cheers went up in thanks and celebration for their safe return. Clouds of bright flower petals rained down upon the men as they marched by their adoring admirers, waving as they passed.

Although their armor was freshly polished and oiled and looked brilliant in the sun, everyone saw how dented and scarred their breastplates, helmets, and shields were. The House flags waved proudly but were poorly stitched and patched by a soldier's hands to repair the sword slashes of the enemy. Most evident to all was the realization of how many were riding in the carts; the wounded and the fallen who would never enter the city again. At the head of the procession rode King Louis, sitting tall and straight on his proud white warhorse. Little did any of the spectators know how much pain the king suffered from his wounds received in the last battle of the campaign. On the king's right hand rode a tall knight bearing the crest of the House of Lion. The people gossiped about what this meant. Is this the one who defended the King? Could he have broken the curse? Would the Lions now rejoin the other Houses with full honor and distinction?

As Jacques approached the reviewing stands where Amanda and the other ladies of the Noble Houses sat, her breath caught in her throat at the sight of him. *Jacques is no longer a boy but a full-grown man! He is proud and tall and strong! Oh, but the look on his face, it is so... serious and sad.* Amanda pushed her senses out to him, privately welcoming him home. He turned and found her in the crowd, giving her a tired smile. *Oh, his eyes are still kind, and I feel the goodness and love still in him. My Jacques is still inside that proud warrior.*

However, with his eyes still on her, she sensed a wave of deep pain, and she understood the reason for his sadness when she saw the wagon following behind the king and his knight. There, placed reverently on the cart surrounded by green boughs and flowers rode the casket containing the remains of Leo, Lord of the House of Lion, covered with the House standard.

Knowing that Amanda sensed the reason for his sorrow, Jacques looked at her and spoke to her in their silent speech. *"Yes, Amanda, he is gone. Struck down by a large knight while fighting next to me. My hand will avenge my father."* With that, he turned his attention back to the road as they passed by the reviewing stand. Amanda could have probed more, but she knew all she needed to know for now, and most importantly, he was finally home.

The homecoming celebration overflowed from the city to the surrounding towns and villages and continued for days until the food and wine finally ran out. The knights and soldiers quickly reunited with their families and sweethearts. Only those who had returned after being long separated from their loved ones could fully appreciate the true joy felt at homecomings like this. Unfortunately, this joy was also tinged with the sorrow of remembering lost family and friends.

For weeks after the celebration, there were different homecoming celebrations as those lost in battle were laid to rest in the Houses of their Ancestors. Amanda stood next to Jacques as Leo's knights carried him into the mausoleum. She cried the tears he would not, feeling the waves of sadness, grief, and a burning desire for revenge radiating off him. She wanted to comfort him but dared not try to reach that place in his heart. They stood as close as they dared with their hands barely touching. Jacques felt the private love Amanda had for him and hoped she felt his love in return. He appreciated what she tried to do, and he wished he knew how to help her reach him, but the grief was still too fresh.

Jacques, now the Head of the House of Lion, spent the next two months learning all his new responsibilities. As much as he desperately missed Amanda, there was no time to roam the forests or visit with her. Every time he started a letter or note to her, some new problem interrupted him and it was forgotten. It was another month before he realized how much time had passed since he had left the chateaux. Setting everything else aside, Jacques decided it was well past time to visit Amanda and spend the day with her as they had before. As he rode to the House of Osprey, he shed the weight of his newly found responsibilities and grief, feeling a lightness of spirit that had eluded him for a long time. He saw one of their bird friends who noisily welcomed him home. Jacques laughed out loud as he thanked the bird and asked it to pass on his greetings to all the Woodland Folk. Jacques was felt like his old self again as he approached Phillip's gates.

Once there, he saw a line of young men from the other Noble Houses milling around outside closed gates. *This is odd,* he thought *Phillip always keeps his gates open as a sign of his hospitality.*

Riding up, the other young men looked at him a little disrespectfully. They did not fully believe the stories of his bravery and did not like that they had to treat him as the head of a fully restored and honored Noble House.

Jacques asked, "What are you doing here? Is someone sick in the House?" They looked at him with disbelief. "Have you not heard? We are here to lay suit and to court Lady Amanda. If that is your intention, get off your horse and get in line!" This time Jacques laughed scornfully and said, "Not likely!" Spurring his horse ahead, Jacques scattered the young nobles on his way to the gates. The guards, recognizing him as Head of the Lions and having heard the disrespect from those not brave enough to fight, opened the gates to allow Jacques alone to enter.

Lord Phillip, having seen and heard what happened, strode out of the chateaux and properly greeted Lord Jacques. With the formalities observed, Phillip gave Jacques a kind smile saying, "I urge caution, my young friend. I understand your feelings, and I know how they treat you. If you accept a little advice, you may need the support of the other nobles some-day. Scattering their sons like geese on the road is not the way to earn their goodwill."

Jacques dropped his head a bit to hide a slight grin and said, "That is wise advice, Phillip. My father gave me similar guidance when I was a boy. Thank you for the reminder." Then remembering the reason for his visit said, "May I ask if Lady Amanda is home, and if so, may I talk with her?"

At that moment, Amanda walked out the door on the arm of the young noble, Lucian, and upon seeing Jacques, her smile vanished, and she turned pale. Then Lucian gave him a sidelong glance, relishing the shocked look on Jacques's face. He boldly gave Amanda a peck on the cheek, saying, "Thank you, my lady. I had a wonderful time today and thank you for promising me the first dance at your father's next party."

She had promised nothing of the kind. She may have liked him a little, but not enough to dance with him or allow him to kiss her cheek! As the noble sauntered away, openly smirking at Jacques, Phillip stood in front of him. "Careful Lucian," he growled in a low and dangerous tone. "You will respect my House, my daughter, and my guests! Or you will no longer be welcome here. Am I clear?" The smirk left the suitor's face as he formally bowed to Phillip, Lady Amanda, and a nod of his head to Jacques. "Leave. NOW!" roared Phillip, determined to speak with the Head of this pipsqueak's House. Calling to the guards, Phillip commanded that no one else be admitted.

An awkward silence blanketed the courtyard. "Let us go inside and talk, son..." Phillip began, but was interrupted by his daughter.

"Lord Jacques," addressing him with an unfamiliar formality. Her eyes filled with tears of anguish, "I...I..." Then, regaining her composure and dignity, she said, "Welcome to our House, Lord. Treat it as your own." Straightening her posture, she walked back into the house, leaving it to her father to explain. As she climbed the stairs, Amanda could not forget the look of shock and betrayal on Jacques's face. She walked to her room and laid on her bed, sobbing into her pillow.

He has to understand! He should understand better than anyone that none of this was my choice! I told him of what life is like as a woman in Aquitaine. With her embarrassment turning to anger. *Besides, who does he think he is only now coming to see me? He should know that a woman should only have to wait so long for a man, even if she has feelings for him! Does he somehow think we made a promise to one another? He could have at least written to me when he got home!* With that, she cried even harder.

Phillip again recognized the formal way his daughter used Jacques's name and understood that this situation was now even more complicated. He had made a promise to the other Houses, but now he had to weigh that promise against the happiness and well-being of his daughter. Again, he pushed the thought away for later and showed Jacques to the Great Room.

Jake put the book down. Tears stung his eyes as the story had become all too real to him. A girl at school who he liked a lot and whom he thought liked him, started going out with one of the popular boys. Every time Jake saw them in the hallway, walking hand-in-hand and laughing was like a punch in the stomach. He was confused by a jumble of feelings: hurt, anger, sadness, and misguided hope that she would smile his way or say "Hi". Unfortunately, that greeting never came, and his heart became heavier.

CHAPTER SIX

Time passed, and Jake grew into an exceptional young man. His grades had improved as did his concentration in class. Jake could now answer the questions he was asked, and he developed a love for writing. He outgrew his clumsiness and was recruited by several of the school's sports teams. Had he been able to look outside himself, Jake would have discovered he was becoming more and more like Jacques. He noticed his taste in music, books, hobbies, and what was important in his social life had changed. He realized that there were other girls he liked who liked him back. Jake took his time to get to know each girl before asking her out. He was shy and unsure of himself. However, when Jake was honest with himself, he knew he was looking for his Amanda, realizing just how rare someone like her was.

It wasn't long before Jake was packing up for the university, looking forward to life in a new city away from Arlington. He wanted to challenge himself, immerse himself in new subjects with new instructors, and meet new people. Most of all, he wanted to learn how to write and become an author. One thing Jake loved to do most was make up stories just to see how they would end.

During his time at university, Jake occasionally picked up the book his uncle had given him and read through certain sections. Lately, it was hard for him to read it all the way through since Uncle Jerry had passed away the year before. Jake often remembered how the two of them would sit in a quiet corner and talk about the way the story seemed to change. During those talks, Jake would always come back to the subject of Lady Amanda. Uncle Jerry would smile at the way Jake described her, understanding how easy she was to like and to love. They both recognized her to be one of the more interesting and complex characters in the book. Amanda was stronger and more intelligent than most of the others and had a soft side, a sensitive side that was easily hurt.

Jake finally asked, "Uncle Jerry, did you love Amanda too?"

"No," his uncle said. "My story happened in Korea with a whole set of different characters. Remember Jake, the book is different for each person who reads it. I don't know how your story will end, but I will tell you this. If you truly love a character in the book, that character will love you back, and the story will become real for you." Jake didn't know what to say to that or even know how such a thing was possible, but he took his uncle at his word. It convinced Jake more than ever that there was something magical about that book.

The last time he sat next to Uncle Jerry's bedside in the hospital, the subject of the book came up again. They talked and laughed for hours about the adventures and characters. Just before Jake left, Uncle Jerry took his hand and held it tight, looking into his eyes and saying, "Jake, remember what I told you. If you love Amanda, she will love you back, and she will become real for you!"

Later that night, Jake got a call from his mom, telling him Uncle Jerry passed away in his sleep. "You must have had some conversation with him, Jake. He passed with such a contented and peaceful smile."

As Jake started his senior year at university, his life changed in a remarkable way. As he and his friend Rick, sat leaning against a tree on campus, Jake's eyes felt heavy and gradually closed. Then a voice with a wonderfully lyrical French accent said, "It's time you woke up sleepyhead!"

Surprised, he jumped to his feet, saying, "I was just resting my eyes."

He wasn't very convincing, and she teased him by saying, "I'm sure you were...désolée; I do not yet know your name."

Jake's roommate, Rick said, "His name is Jake, and in case you couldn't tell, he is delighted to meet you too."

She gave Jake a brilliant smile and winked, saying, "Enchanté, Jacques. My name is Amandine Auvergne, but you may call me Manda." As their fingers touched on shaking hands, there was a tiny spark like a static charge, and Manda went on; "It is a pleasure to meet such a polite young man. Perhaps we will see each other again soon."

As they watched Amandine walk away, Rick put his arm around Jake's shoulders and said, "Buddy, you have all the luck!"

The next day, Jake found out that Amandine was in many of his classes, studying a year abroad at the university. He noticed Manda had no trouble keeping up in any of the classes even though she was a year behind and studying in a second language. As they talked, he discovered they laughed at the same jokes and listened to similar types of music. Since they were part of the same study group, the two of them spent a lot of time together learning more about the subject and each other. Jake couldn't help noticing her long dark hair and green eyes. From the beginning, he knew her obvious beauty wasn't what drew him to her. There was something deeper. Her intelligence and free and open spirit told him there was more to this exceptional young woman than met the eye. Jake knew she reminded him of someone, but he couldn't quite put his finger on it.

Soon, Jake and Manda started to date and after a while, they became serious about each other. She told him of her life in France, describing the chateaux her family had owned for generations. It was large and had many windows to let in the sunlight. A grand staircase dominated the foyer, and it had a wonderful library with both old and new books on many subjects. Manda also told Jake about the grand ballroom where her parents often entertained. She said she preferred smaller parties with gatherings of four or five. Jake told her about the small town he'd grown up in and about Uncle Jerry's library. He told her how much he loved reading and his secret desire to write a book. He told Manda about the one special book he'd been given as a gift years before. At first, Jake thought she would think him silly or even a little nutty for thinking a book was growing up with him, but she didn't think that at all.

Manda said, "There is much in this world we don't understand. We would be arrogant to believe just because we can't explain it doesn't mean it isn't true."

Jake loved the long talks he had with Manda. She had a quick mind and a wonderfully wicked sense of humor. He had to admit that he loved the sound of her voice and laughter. They spent hours talking, and since he had spent his whole life in a small town, Jake wanted to hear her opinions on all different topics. Coming from two different countries, they often had differing views on things like politics, literature, world events, and life in the United States. Most of the time, they enjoyed hearing each other's thoughts. Sometimes though, the discussions would become heated, and they would debate late into the night. Jake came to love how her eyes flashed when she felt strongly about something.

Manda also had this way of reading people and knowing whether they were trustworthy. However, one of the most unusual traits she had was her innate connection with animals. It was almost as if they understood each other. When she stayed with Jake's family at Christmas, Jake's dog completely ignored him and wouldn't leave Manda's side. The dog even slept in the bed with her at night. Manda was the most remarkable woman Jake had ever known, and he realized he was falling in love with her.

The year passed quickly, and with graduation, just two months away, both Jake and Manda knew she would return to France soon to finish her last year of university. They would walk hand-in-hand or sit close to each other on a park bench knowing the separation would be difficult for them, making plans to visit each other as often as possible.

Manda stayed on for another couple of weeks after Jake's graduation. They spent every day together, sometimes wandering the woods surrounding his town or driving to Chicago to visit museums and concerts. They knew their time was precious, and they didn't waste a moment. One rainy day they spent all morning walking around, arriving home later that day soaked to the skin with Manda laughing at how Jake's hair looked when wet.

The day before Manda was to leave for home; they had a picnic in a meadow close to Jake's house. It was a warm day, and Jake laid down with his head on Manda's lap. She softly sang a sad song in French to him while she played with his hair.

"Jacques, your hair is being most unreasonable today," she laughed.

Jake said, "It is most unreasonable every day." Sitting up, Jake kissed her and told Manda how he felt about her, and how he wished he could go with her. Manda said she felt the same way and began to cry, saying how much she would miss him. Later that night, Jake's parents hosted a Bon Voyage party for Manda that went late into the night. The next day; Manda was gone.

Over the next several months, Jake and Amandine wrote letters and called each other constantly. Jake began working as a history teacher at his old high school to earn money to pay for the master's program he planned to take and for plane fare to France.

It was taking him longer than he expected and he was constantly apologizing to Manda for the delay. Over time, Jake noticed subtle changes in how often Manda wrote. There was a growing formality in the language. At first, he thought it his imagination and spoke to his mom about it. She tried to calm his mind, but said finally, "Jake, if it concerns you, ask her about it."

Finally, he worked up the courage and asked her in one of their phone conversations. She admitted that things had changed a little because he wasn't there. Her parents said that while they liked Jake well enough, they thought it would be better if she started dating local boys, so she was sure about her feelings. Jake sat on the other end of the line in silence, not knowing what to say. Manda promised she would call him in two days, but she got busy and they never spoke. The same thing happened the next week. They still wrote, but even that became inconsistent. To take his mind off Manda, he picked a book at random from his bookcase. It vibrated in his hand. Jake knew, without looking at the cover, it was the right choice.

Chapter Seven

Decisions

Phillip carefully watched Jacques as he walked to the great room. He saw the confusion on the young Lord's face and the tension in his shoulders. Offering Jacques a seat by the fireplace, Phillip walked over to a cabinet and poured them both a glass of strong port wine. He gave Jacques one glass and sat down in a chair opposite the young lord, waiting for him to speak.

"I, I don't understand what is happening, Phillip," Jacques finally said. "I thought Amanda and I had an understanding. We never spoke of it out loud, but it was always obvious to me that one day…" His voice trailed off into silence. Jacques took a drink of the port, and as the wine warmed his chest, he felt something break loose in his heart. Words and feelings he had never spoken came tumbling out in a torrent. He spoke of living under the shadow of the unwarranted shame that covered both his House and his childhood. Of how he endured the insults and betrayals of his former friends and how that virtually shaped every relationship he'd had had since then. He told Phillip of how that changed once he met Amanda, who treated him with genuine kindness. She never once looked down on him, and for the first time in his young life, he had someone with whom he could laugh and share his most private thoughts. Amanda had listened to all his hopes and dreams without laughing or criticizing, but she could also tell him when she thought he was wrong about something. Amanda was the first person who told him she believed in him and who had given him complete loyalty, honesty, and respect. She saw him when everyone else chose not to.

Jacques then spoke of the battles fought during the rebellion, of the blood, horror, and loss of many good men whom he respected and loved like brothers. With great effort, he told Phillip of the last battle. Of, how Jacques and Leo fought side-by-side when the king was struck down. Without thinking, Jacques had run to King Louis and stood over him, driving the rebels back. To Jacques's right, he'd watched his father fighting as fiercely as a man half his age. Leo had looked at Jacques with a savage grin that spoke of a father's love and a warrior's respect.

Then, a huge Ignominia Knight in black armor had attacked Leo with a ferocity that drove him back. As Jacques defended the king, he'd watched helplessly while Leo's shield shattered, leaving him defenseless to the killing blow that came next. Then the knight, whom he later heard was named Morlok, stood over Leo and roared in victory, hacking at his lifeless body. Looking over at Jacques with hatred and battle-lust, Morlok had been ready to attack when the Ignominia's trumpets sounded a retreat. Morlok had pointed his sword at Jacques and said, "We will meet again, and on that day, I will take everything from you!" With that, he'd joined his fellow rebels withdrawing from the field.

Jacques put his face in his hands and wept.

Phillip now understood why the praises of King Louis meant so little to the young lord. For Jacques, loyalty was absolute, and in defending his king, Jacques felt he had carried out the ultimate act of betrayal by not coming to his father's aid. Because of this, he had isolated himself behind a wall of new responsibilities, feeling unworthy of his title and perhaps even Amanda's love. Having fought many battles himself, Phillip intimately understood the chaos of battle that forced warriors to make snap decisions and sacrifices. Jacques strained under the weight of the burden of misplaced guilt. Leo would not have felt betrayed, and in fact, would have felt a new level of pride and respect for Jacques's choice. Jacques had stood between the king's death and the death of Aquitaine. However, Phillip knew only time would convince the young lord of this truth.

For the first time since sitting down, Phillip spoke. In a soft voice, barely heard above the crackling fire, he said, "Have courage, Jacques! You are destined for greatness, although that means nothing to you now. Before you left to fight the rebellion, your father told me of how proud he was of you. Leo said, 'I could not have had a better son! I was hard on him while he was young only because I do not know how to be anything else. I depended on Amélie to show him the love I could not, but look at him, Phillip! I know he will prove himself in battle! There is no one I trust more than Jacques, and I am convinced he will not fail his king or Aquitaine. I have never told him this, it's never been my way, but I love that boy!" Phillip let those words hang in the air, allowing Jacques to hear and absorb their importance.

After a time, Phillip spoke again. "I ask that you do not judge Amanda. You know the customs here as well as I do and none of us can avoid them without heaping dishonor on her. It has been a long-held practice that we give every daughter of a Noble House a chance to be courted by the sons of the other Houses. This custom, while archaic, has a purpose. It allows the Houses to form alliances that would be impossible outside of familial ties. If these ties did not exist, there would be constant bickering between the Houses, leading to open violence." Phillip shook his head. "While I find the practice of putting my daughter on display repugnant, I am subject to the same laws and customs as are you. Maybe your generation will find a better way, but for now, I have given my word as Lord of the House of Osprey, and my word is my bond!"

Jacques looked at Phillip with sad but peaceful eyes and said, "Thank you, Philip, for listening to my story with an open heart and mind. Thank you, too, for telling me of my father's devotion and love for me. It eases my mind some." His eyes dropped to the empty hands in his lap, and he said, "You have given me the proper reminder of how our customs have shaped our lives for generations and the importance of them, especially as I take on the mantle of lord of my House. As you spoke, it reminded me of Amanda, telling me of what a woman's life is like and how she dreaded this custom. I realize now that I have only seen things as I wished them to be, not as they are. I regret to say that I have taken Amanda's feelings for granted, and I must apologize to her for that."

Feeling a renewed sense of respect for Jacques, Phillip thought, *I've not heard any of the other young Nobles talk about Amanda in this way. To them, she is a possession to be negotiated for. Jacques sees Amanda for who she is and that she is to be respected and loved. He must have true feelings for her.*

"Give her time lad," Phillip said. "You two have been inseparable for these past years. Amanda needs to be sure of her feelings for you. She has never talked to another boy as much as she has to you. Besides, neither of you have spent much time with the young people of the other Houses. It may not seem like it now, but this will be good for both of you. How can you know what love is until you know what it is not?"

Jacques slowly nodded his head as he stood straight and proud. He said, "Lord Phillip, I ask your permission to sometime soon walk and talk with Lady Amanda in hopes of being her choice to be courted."

Phillip smiled and shook Jacques's hand. "Nothing would make me happier, Lord Jacques!"

How can you know what love is until you know what it is not? Jake reread that sentence until he saw it with his eyes closed. Jake now understood what he had to do, and for the first time in days, he had hope.

CHAPTER EIGHT

Although the story took place in the Twelfth Century, Jake thought the situation was still the same. He had taken certain things for granted with Manda and assumed their relationship would stay the same. He recognized he had never officially met her parents, so they didn't know what kind of man he was. Jake had unintentionally put her in the awkward position of having to defend her feelings for him to her parents. He also realized the rudeness of having not learning the French language. It was then that Jake did everything he could to show Manda's parents who he was and how deeply he loved their daughter. Jake started right away by arranging for private lessons with the French teacher at the high school so he could speak to Manda's parents without her having to interpret. Jake also tutored students and worked side jobs to make enough money to travel to France as soon as possible. Last, Jake sent handwritten letters to Manda, sometimes using the words she had taught him (she always laughed when he tried to use them in a conversation), telling her about his life and plans. Jake tried not to worry about her irregular responses. He kept telling himself, *How can you know what love is until you know what it is not?* Jake even went on a few dates himself to see if his feelings had changed, only to discover they had not.

When he had enough money saved up, he telephoned Manda and asked if he could come to visit her. She seemed reluctant. She said she would ask her parents how they felt about it and to let him know. Manda called back the next day telling him her parents were eager to meet him. He was excited as he made his flight arrangements, and Jake worked extra hard on his French lessons so he could at least carry on a short conversation with her parents. He also learned as much as he could about Bordeaux and some history of the region where Manda and her family lived. It surprised Jake to learn the region used to be called Aquitaine and her family had lived near Bordeaux for hundreds of years.

He remembered his uncle's words, "If you truly love a character in the book, they will truly love you back and the story will become real for you." Jake pushed the idea away, telling himself some things were just too fanciful to believe.

As the day of the flight arrived, Jake was a wreck and all his fears came tumbling out.

"What if she has met someone else? What if her parents hate me? What if…?"

"Everything works out?" his mom interrupted.

Jake had to laugh at that. As he hugged his mom goodbye, she said, "Just be yourself. That's the person she originally fell for." Jake had to admit it was good advice and he tried to relax and enjoy the flight.

Throughout the long flight, Jake kept practicing the greeting to Amandine's parents. An older woman with a kind face turned to him and said, "She must be very special to you, that you are practicing the greeting to her parents so diligently." With an embarrassed grin Jake admitted she was and introduced himself. The woman asked him to please call her Amélie.

Jake felt an immediate connection to this woman as he briefly told her about Manda and what had recently happened, ending with, "Amandine is everything to me."

Smiling, she said, "Well then, Jacques, let us be sure you get this right! As we say in France, Ce n'est pas la mer à boire." Seeing Jake's eyes widen in panic, she laughed and added, "It means, it's not as if you have to drink the sea." Jake looked more confused than ever, but she explained, "This means you are making this too hard. Let me help make it easier for you." For the rest of the flight, Amélie worked with Jake on his pronunciation and delivery.

As they landed, Amélie laid a warm hand on his arm and said, "I hope you will allow one last piece of advice from this old woman. Impossible n'est pas Français. It means impossible isn't French. Jacques, mon ami, we French see nothing as impossible. Especially in love, nothing is impossible." With that, she gave Jake a kiss on both cheeks and slowly left the plane.

When he got to baggage claim, he saw Manda's beautiful smile, and all the butterflies in his stomach disappeared. She gave Jake a quick hug and a peck on both cheeks, introducing him to her parents.

They said in English, "Hello, Jacques. It is a pleasure to meet you."

Jake cleared his throat and said, "Bonjour, Monsieur et Madame Auvergne. Je suis heureux de vous rencontrer." Manda stared wide-eyed at Jake in shock. Jake whispered to Manda, "Did I say something wrong?"

Her parents clapped their hands in delight and said, "Non, Jacques. You said it perfectly! Come, let us hurry home. We have much to talk about while you are with us."

As they headed for the airport exit, Jake saw Amélie looking over at the happy little group. She gave him a smile and a little wave. As Jake waved back, he turned to Manda to point her out, but when he looked back, she was gone. *I don't understand, she was just there, and she doesn't walk that fast.*

Just then, Manda said something and, with Amélie's words "impossible isn't French" echoing in his mind, he turned all his attention to her.

Chapter Nine

A New Beginning

Once Jacques left the chateaux, Phillip made his way to Amanda's room. He called her name as he knocked on the heavy oaken door and waited for her answer. After a few moments, he heard her faint voice telling him to come in. As he entered her bedroom, it surprised Phillip to see Amanda, her eyes red and angry. Yet she appeared composed

"Amanda..." he began, but she held up her hand. Surprised, he cocked his head and looked at her, waiting for her to speak.

"Father, I don't want to hear anything HE had to say! How dare he ride here after ignoring me for all these months! Did he expect me to run to him like some common serving girl? I will NOT be treated this way, and father, you should not allow it! Lord Jacques thinks more of himself than he should and forgets that I, too am of noble birth and a royal line!"

Phillip waited and listened for some time as his daughter's anger spent itself. He knew much of what she felt was true, but much more of it was one-sided. Philip saw Amanda expected much more from Jacques than all the other nobles, and it was hard for her to imagine how a year-and-a-half of war changes a man.

Yes, Jacques took some things for granted. Yes, he was at times overly proud, but so was Amanda. Jacques was young, and as Phillip remembered his youth, he was much the same way. Yes, many of the things Jacques said didn't come out as he intended, but it was clear from their conversation that Jacques respected and cared for Amanda in a way that none of the other nobles did. Phillip also recognized that the lad had intelligence, substance, and the ability and desire to grow into a man he would be proud to know. Still, Phillip knew his daughter well enough to know that none of this mattered right now. He had to let her come to her conclusions concerning Jacques in her own time, and it was best to let this conversation be for now. The one thing he knew to be true was that Amanda must care for Jacques a great deal for her to be this hurt and angry at him.

Over the next few months, there was little outward change in Amanda's attitude towards Jacques. If they met on the street, she was polite, but always had to be somewhere else to meet with another one of her suitors. He was equally polite, keeping his face impassive. During these encounters, Jacques seethed with jealousy while Amanda felt heartbroken that he seemed unconcerned with her seeing someone else. It was a game they both played poorly and one they were both losing. The other young nobles were delighted at this change in attitude towards the upstart Lion and tried to take advantage of the situation by subtly whispering half-truths and innuendos about Jacques's character to her. However, all that did was make her angrier because Amanda, more than anyone else, recognized the clumsy lies, reflecting the poor character of the nobles.

After every encounter with Amanda, Jacques would go back to those activities that had previously brought him peace and joy. However, when he read, he would come across subjects he would want to talk about with Amanda. He tried riding his horse, Charger, but it would remind him of Amanda so he stopped. Every time Jacques entered the stable, Charger, would stamp and greet him, tossing his head towards the tack room. Jacques would only rest his head on the diamond on Charger's forehead, scratch behind his ears, and breathe in the horse's earthy scent. Then Jacques, having no one else to talk to, would pour out all his feelings to his old friend. The horse sensing the sadness in his master stood still, nickering in sympathy, and gently rubbing his head against Jacques.

Jacques would wander the forest visiting the secret places he and Amanda discovered, but inevitably he would remember a time of laughter and wonder with her. When he would meet one of the Woodland Folk, they would run up to him with excited greetings and look for Amanda. Jacques did the best he could to be happy to see them, but he could not find it in himself. That part of him was gone, and the creatures could feel an overwhelming sense of loss. They did their best to ease his pain.

Jacques would take out a pen and paper to write Amanda letters, but they always ended up in a crumpled ball on the floor. One night, he wrote a poem to her, as he had in the past. After several mis-starts, he wrote:

You are a star.
A diamond burning in the inky darkness.
You are bright.
You are beautiful.
You are steadfast.
You are pure light and pure love.
Tonight, you are far away.
Beyond my embrace.
Still, your light guides me home.

"Yes, Amanda," he said to the darkness beyond the candlelight. "You are far away and beyond my embrace. It seems your star shines for someone else tonight."

For her part, Amanda quickly learned not to share her special abilities with the other nobles. Instead, she would take them into the forest and try to share the magic of the place with them. They would yawn and begin to talk about some impressive deed they had accomplished or sing loudly to break their unease at the quiet. Sometimes, she sensed the nobles were trying to remember the paths they took so they could return with their friends and hunt the woodland creatures. Knowing this, Amanda always took a different and more confusing route every time they walked the paths.

Other times, she tried to share some new or interesting ideas with them. More often than not, they would get angry and tell her she was trying to make them feel inferior. They would say things like, "Girls have no business getting an education!" or "I don't know why you read so much. Everyone knows it's a waste of time."

Confused, Amanda would say that wasn't the case at all that she wanted to get to know them better. Unfortunately, her candor only offended them further, and she would give them an apology she neither felt nor meant. It was an awkward and confusing time for Jacques and Amanda. Both deeply missed each other, but they could not find their way back to where they wanted to be.

Finally, Amanda went to Phillip to ask for his advice on what to do. All the Houses were pressuring her for a decision.

All the Houses but one.

Her father sat her down and told her he understood why she had been upset earlier. He understood her confusion now. He then spoke of how impressed he was by Jacques's character and how deeply Jacques cared for her. When Amanda tried to protest this, he told her about the conversation he'd had with Jacques. Phillip talked of Jacques's confusion about the situation and how it was compounded by being an outcast for so long and having little experience with polite society. He told her about how Jacques felt about her and the deep respect he had for her. Philip shared what Jacques could not concerning the war, speaking of the horrors Jacques had faced in battle and of the sense of loss and betrayal he felt concerning the death of his father. Amanda felt the hot tears silently stream down her face when she realized how badly the two of them had misread each other's actions. She thought, we know each other so well and yet not as we should.

Phillip finished by telling her how he explained the agreement he made with the other Houses and how he was honor-bound to keep his word. Last, Philip told Amanda of how Jacques, now fully understanding the situation, asked to talk with Amanda, hoping to court her.

"He said that?" Amanda said, confused. "I do not understand. Every time I see Jacques, he's so formal, so polite, and so infuriatingly cold!" "How did you expect him to act?" Phillip asked. "Every time you saw him, you were always running off to see another noble. Then, when you knew he saw you with someone else, you always laughed a little harder and held their arm a little tighter. He respected your situation and your interest in others!"

After that conversation, the ice slowly started to thaw between Jacques and Amanda. They realized that they had both matured and changed since he'd left for war. They resolved to take the time to re-discover each other again. They still cared a great deal for each other, but they resolved together to make a new beginning. They wanted their relationship to grow past a childhood affection to adult love.

The change in their relationship was noticeable to all who saw them, including the jilted nobles. People often saw Jacques and Amanda walking together deep in conversation or off riding to secret places. Jacques had newfound confidence with his peers and no longer felt the weight of his past. The young couple developed a reputation for always laughing together, sometimes so hard they had to wipe away each other's tears. He listened closely to Amanda, and his admiration and deep affection for her grew. They did not argue as much as having long discussions about topics important to them. Each one would probe the other's opinions out of genuine interest for their views.

Amanda now felt she had found a man who fully accepted her for who she was and not what he title could offer him. The thing that pleased Amanda the most was Jacques' respect for her. He treated her like an equal (sometimes even deferring to her) in plain sight of everyone. When they both knew their love was true, Amanda and Jacques promised themselves to each other, much to the delight of most of the people of Bordeaux.

On the first day of spring, Jacques arrived at Phillip's Chateaux dressed in a new formal outfit asking to speak with Phillip on an important matter. Jacques could not remember ever feeling this nervous. The sweat ran down his back. He marched into the great room, behaving so formal and so terrified Phillip had to bite his lip to keep from smiling.

Jacques started by saying, "Lord Phillip, you…ah…err, know how much I love and um care for the Lady Amanda. She is, ahem, everything I have ever, um, looked for… err that is, ahhhhhh…."

Phillip couldn't hold back anymore. Laughing he said, "Of course you have my blessing to ask Amanda to marry! I was afraid if I let you go on like that, you would not have finished asking by the winter." Clapping Jacques on the back, Phillip added, "Now you better go ask her before I change my mind!" Jacques gave him a terrified look that set Phillip into more fits of laughter. "Go, go," he wheezed, "tell the servant you need to talk with the Lady. Hahahahahahahaha."

With the servant on her errand, Phillip excused himself so Jacques and Amanda could be alone. "Remember lad, simpler is always better with things like this." he said over his shoulder. "I'll be back in an hour in case you get stuck."

Jacques could hear the echoes of Phillip's laughter as he walked down the hall to the library. Amanda came walking into the room, bewildered by what had gotten into her father, but with one look at Jacques, standing straight, tall, and handsome, she had her answer, and her knees started to shake.

"Amanda, my beloved, your name means 'worthy of great love,' and those words describe you perfectly. Since the day we met, I've recognized you were like no one I've ever known. As soon as I think I know all there is to know about you, you surprise me with something new. Every day, I see a new facet of your beauty, grace, compassion, courage, and intelligence. Amanda, you make me laugh as no one else has, and you make me want to dance. With you, I forget my cares because together, I am convinced nothing is impossible. I have been blessed by having you in my life. Amanda dearest, you have shown me what true love is."

He then got down on one knee and took out his mother's ring. He said, "Amanda, please marry me."

Amanda, with tears in her eyes, sank to her knees with him saying, "With all my heart, YES Jacques! I will marry you."

With trembling hands, Jacques placed the ring on her shaking finger, and for the first time, they kissed. When Phillip found them, they were in each other's arms, foreheads touching. They were crying and laughing at the same time.

With a big grin on his face, Phillip congratulated the happy couple and said, "As I said lad, simpler is better!"

CHAPTER TEN

J ake spent a month with Manda and her parents at their ancestral chateaux. He took his time in learning about their family history and the history of France and Bordeaux. He did all he could to experience the food and culture. The Auvergnes were impressed by this young American. Not only had he traveled to France to meet them, but he also made every effort to get to know them. They saw that, unlike the tourists who flocked to Bordeaux every summer, he was open to all he experienced. Manda and Jake walked arm in arm all over Bordeaux. They visited little shops, stopped to listen to sidewalk musicians, visited museums, and sat in the sidewalk cafes drinking coffee, making up funny stories about the people walking by.

The young couple also spent much of their time alone, getting to know each other again and learn about the new and exciting things happening in their lives. Jake apologized to Manda for the mistakes he had made with her, chief among them was taking her and their relationship for granted. He admitted that they had changed over the last year and he asked if they could start over again, like the first time they were together. Manda also admitted her mistakes and apologized. She said she should have been more honest with Jake about what her parents wanted and how scared she felt being so attached to someone living so far away. Manda had missed sitting next to Jake with his arm around her, or the walks they had shared while holding hands. It had been easier to move on in his absence rather than hurt as she had. Jake saw she was much more at ease Bordeaux and asked her to teach him more French.

As Manda worked on his pronunciation, they laughed and made fun of his accent. It was almost as if they were learning a secret language only the two of them could understand, but soon the vendors in the market stalls and stores could understand him, and enjoyed the short, simple conversations with Jake.

As the time to return to America approached, Jake recognized how lonely life would be in the coming months without Manda near him. Knowing that every moment they spent together was precious, he spent as much time as he could with her, memorizing the sound of her voice, the smell of her hair, how her eyes crinkled when she laughed, and how her warm hand felt in his. Manda's parents noticed the change in their daughter, especially how happy and content she was with Jake. They began to see what Amandine saw in Jake, and their objections disappeared one by one. During their final family dinner, Mr. Auvergne told them he and his wife were grateful Jake had come to France and now after getting to know him, they were no longer opposed to Amandine and Jake seeing each other. The Auvergne's announced they would like to visit Jake and his parents later on that year, and Jake said they would be welcome anytime.

Before he left France, Jake and Manda agreed that this time they would do things differently while they were apart. They promised to be honest about the things bothering them and to not take anything for granted. At the airport, they held each other in a long embrace, softly telling each other how they felt, and wiping each other's tears away. Jake kissed Manda and told her he loved her, picked up his bag, and walked to his gate. Jake fought his emotions all the way home, feeling sad to leave a big part of himself behind but also overjoyed at how bright their future looked.

As he sat at his gate, he smiled hearing Amélie's voice whisper, *Impossible isn't French.* He couldn't wait to tell his parents everything.

This time, things between the two of them were different, and despite the distance, they grew closer. As the time for Manda and her parents' visit got closer, Jake became fanatical about making sure everything was just right. This included the kinds of food they served their guests and what the Auvergne's would do for fun while they were in America. His parents were mostly good-natured about his behavior admitting they had never seen him like this before. They were, however, able to convince him that a list of daily activities was probably too much. He needed to let their visitors choose what they'd like to do and see.

Jake and his parents met the Auvergne's at the airport. Jake and Manda had done such a good job of telling their parents about each other, the first meeting was like greeting old friends. Both sets of parents quickly fell into a comfortable friendship and good-natured discussions about the merits of their home countries. While in America, Jake and his parents introduced the Auvergne's to barbecue (interesting), baseball (confusing), hot dogs with mustard (they politely ate, declining seconds), and to what life was like in a small American town (charming AND relaxing).

One afternoon, Jake and Mr. Auvergne were walking in the woods and talking about what Amandine meant to each of them.

"Sir," Jake said, "the months I've known Amandine have been the happiest of my life. It's hard to remember what life was like before we met, and every day I discover something new about her. She is the most loving and gracious person I know, and she has filled my life with joy. I am a better man for having known her, and I want to spend the rest of my life with her. Mr. Auvergne, may I have your permission to ask her to marry me?"

"Of course, Jacques!" her father said, enthusiastically clapping Jake on the back. "When you visited us, Amandine's mother and I agreed you two would be the perfect match! I have only one suggestion though. We have an old family saying with things like this, 'Remember, simpler is always better.'"

Late one evening, after everyone else had gone to bed, Manda and Jake were sitting by the fireplace talking softly. Jake took a deep breath and said, "Amandine, I am so happy you are in my life, and when we are apart, my memories of our time together…"

"Jacques, I have something to say first," Manda said, interrupting him. "It is the most important thing I've ever said to anyone. Jacques dearest, I too realize how much I need you in my life. I have known no one like you. You are smart, funny, and handsome. You see me. Not just the outside, but you see all of me. No one has ever loved me as completely or unconditionally as you have." Manda paused, taking an ancient and scarred family heirloom ring from a pocket. She slipped it on his left hand, saying, "Jacques mon amour, veux-tu m'épouser?"

Jake looked at her, confused as he worked through the translation. Slowly, as the words formed in his mind, he smiled saying, "Yes, Manda, I will marry you." Then taking his Grandmother's ring from his pocket, he slipped it on to her left ring finger and said, "Amandine, will you marry me?"

"Oui, oui mon amour!"

Chapter Eleven

The Royal Court

*I*t was Phillip's happy duty to announce the engagement of his daughter, the Lady Amanda of House Osprey to Lord Jacques of House Lion at a celebration larger than any in anyone's memory. King Louis and his royal court received an invitation as did all the nobles from the various Houses. Tables and benches took up most of the open space in the chateaux, the courtyard, and gardens, and only the richest of foods and the finest wines were served to his guests. All day and night, toasts, announcements, pronouncements, congratulations, and swearing of allegiances were made. It was all a blur to Jacques and Amanda. The sheer number of good wishes they received overwhelmed them. Afterward, it was hard to remember much of the party.

The couple also realized this party would be small compared to the wedding celebration Phillip was sure to hold in their honor. Several of Jacques's former rivals and past tormentors gathered in the back, muttering and gossiping among themselves as they stuffed their faces with the free food and drink. Jacques was oblivious to all of it, having eyes only for Amanda. After the guests finished dinner, Chancellor Gregory, King Louis' closest advisor, approached Jacques, telling him the King commanded his presence to a private audience tomorrow morning at ten o'clock. He told him not to share this news with anyone. After Jacques acknowledged the summons and the advisor left, he felt both excited and apprehensive as to what this meant. Later, he sat deep in thought, oblivious to everything around him. Amanda called his name, and he didn't respond.

On the third try, she walked up and shook him, saying, "Wake up sleepyhead! It is time to say goodbye to our guests."

The next day, Lord Jacques arrived at the King's Court, right at the last strike of the bell and bowed to King Louis.

"Ah, Lord Jacques, you are punctual as ever," He said giving a sidelong glance at the knot of men in expensive robes and badges of office. "Our other advisors and counselors would do well to follow your example." A shuffling of feet and an embarrassing examination of the floor by some advisors followed this statement, but others looked with disdain and open hostility at Jacques.

I wonder what that's all about. His attention was brought back as the King started addressing him again.

"Lord Jacques, we are impressed with how quickly you have mastered the duties of your House. Ever since the last battle with the Ignominia, we have had a growing concern that there is a lack of decisiveness, cleverness, and dare we say loyalty to the Crown among our advisors and counselors." A chorus of protests rose from the little knot silenced by a look from the King. "Therefore, Lord Jacques, we are naming you Our Royal Chancellor to the Court of Aquitaine. We will discuss your duties in private, but for now, know that you are one of our most trusted advisors." Looking at the group of advisors, the king said, "We dismiss you. We have much to discuss with the young Lion."

Humiliated, the nobles left the room, some glaring at Jacques.

Jacques followed King Louis into his private chambers, and once they were alone, he saw the king's shoulders droop as he began to limp. As the king sat in a cushioned chair and removed his crown, Jacques noticed how grey and straw-like the king's hair had become. In the year since the end of the rebellion, it seemed King Louis had aged ten.

The king saw the look on Jacques's face before he could hide it, and he smiled ruefully, saying in a more informal tone, "Yes, Lord Jacques, I also see what you do when I look in the mirror." Pointing to the Royal Court Chambers he said, "In there I am King of Aquitaine! In here, I am a man, nearly broken by the Ignominia. It would be dangerous to allow that pack of wolves to see their king in this state. They would band together and pull me down like an elk in the forest. That is why you are here. You and Leo were the only nobles who stood by me in my time of greatest need, and it cost you dearly, did it not Lord Jacques?" Jacques could only nod. "Yes, I know it did, and I honor your father for raising a son such as you. Lord Jacques, not only are you one of my finest warriors, but you have also showed great courage, wisdom, and loyalty to me, but more importantly, to Aquitaine."

The king coughed from deep inside his chest and continued. "I know about the injustice you suffered as a lad and how you endured it without flinching. I watched as you grew in stature and intelligence by learning to read and write. Those others," he waved vaguely at the door shaking his head, "they think it unmanly to pick up a book or write their name, so they never learned how. However, not only did you learn to read, but you learned from what you read! You have proven all the qualities and characteristics of one with royal lineage."

"As you know, I never found the time to marry and have children to carry on my line. I have been searching far and wide for a suitable heir and have found no one, not one until now. Lord Jacques, I have named you my heir to the throne. No one knows of this other than Chancellor Gregory, who has prepared the royal proclamation. He is wise and fiercely loyal. You will find that you will need men like him near you to give you counsel on the best course of action. In doing so, you will not swing wide the door to open contempt from and rebellion of the other Houses. I know you will rule with a fair hand, but at times, that hand must be clothed in steel."

The king began to cough violently, and Jacques poured a glass of wine, and kneeling before him and giving it to his Lord.

"Sire, I do not deserve this honor you give me. Ruling Aquitaine is nothing I have aspired to or desired. I am unworthy to take your place."

King Louis smiled and said, "That is what I hoped you would say. That is the attitude of a true king! Yes, you are unprepared, but you are willing and able to learn! You are wise beyond your years and are unafraid to show compassion to the weak. However, you also have something even greater, or should I say, someone. You will have the Lady Amanda by your side. She will be your most loyal and trustworthy companion in your rule as king, and in your life. You, your House, and all of Aquitaine will be blessed because of her!"

A soft knock sounded at the door. "Enter Gregory," said the king, "come and officially greet Aquitaine's future king!" As the king coughed again, Gregory gave him a glass of medicine to drink.

"The honor is mine young Sire," Gregory said. "If it is convenient, shall you and I discuss your duties tomorrow at the same time? Until the proclamation announcement, they must not see you with the king more than necessary. No one can suspect any of this. Otherwise, the other Houses will move to stop it. If I may make a suggestion Sire, tell only Lord Phillip and the Lady Amanda as she will be the one most affected by this new development. They will be your closest and wisest allies. Now if you please, the king is tired and needs rest."

Nodding dumbly, Jacques bowed deeply to the king and said, "I hope it will be many years before my time on the throne comes. Chancellor Gregory, I will see you tomorrow." Bowing again, Jacques left the king's private chambers with a newfound weight on his shoulders.

CHAPTER TWELVE

J ake woke up early to surprise everyone with an engagement celebration breakfast. He was working through the menu in his mind when he smelled coffee brewing. Walking into the kitchen, he saw Manda had the same idea and had planned a much better menu. Together they divided up the different dishes, and soon, a delicious French/American breakfast was on the table when the parents came into the dining room. Manda and Jake made their announcement, and the mothers hugged and cried while the fathers pumped each other's hands, misty-eyed at the news. The happy couple sat in a daze thinking about when and where they would marry, and where their future together would take them.

The next few weeks and months were a blur of wedding preparations. Manda and Jake decided early on that the wedding would take place on the first day of spring the following year. It would be a modest wedding held in France at the small chapel at the family's chateaux. Jake talked with Manda and his parents about where he wanted to complete his Master's degree in history. Before the engagement, the plan was to attend the same university where he graduated with his Bachelor's degree. However, he would now attend an international university near Bordeaux where classes were taught in both French and English. Jake explained he wanted not only to study history but to become immersed in it and France was a perfect place for that.

Jake also told them he wanted to write his own stories and books. He thought this move would give him a larger perspective from which to do that. His parents were a little sad they wouldn't be able to see him as much, but they knew this was the right move for both Jake and Manda.

"Jake, you have always talked about living and working in a different country. What a wonderful opportunity for you to learn about our world and to live your dreams with this amazing woman!" his mom said.

"I agree, son," said his dad. "If you don't do this now, when will you ever do it? It's time to live your lives on your terms and make a future for yourselves!"

Sometimes, the months before the wedding dragged on as if the day would never arrive. Other times, the weeks flew by, and the couple feared they wouldn't get everything done. Not only did they have to plan and complete the wedding arrangements, but there were all the arrangements to make as Jake moved to France. He was accepted into the Master's Program in History at the university, but he still had to get a student visa and find housing. In the meantime, Jake took intensive French language lessons with his tutor, leaving very little time for class preparation.

As he packed and repacked his belongings, Jake made sure he had room for the precious little book his uncle gave him so long ago. The days before leaving, Jake said goodbye to all those who meant so much to him growing up. On the day of his departure, he woke early and walked around the town by himself, silently saying farewell to a place that in recent years had become so dear to him. The ride to the airport with his parents was quiet, with all of them lost in their thoughts. After they parked the car in the departure lane, Jake looked at his parents, not knowing what to say. As always, his dad told a bad joke to break the mood, and they hugged saying goodbye, knowing they would see each other soon at the wedding.

After arriving in France and registering for his classes, Jake threw himself into his studies. His professors soon noticed this serious American who was always ready to discuss the readings for the day. They also noted his language skills had improved, not realizing Manda and her parents only spoke French with him. Soon, Jake's professors were offering him fellowship and research opportunities, much to the disappointment of his fellow students who thought Jake should wait his turn at the back of the academic line.

It wasn't long before Jake's work mysteriously disappeared from his messenger bag. Sometimes when he would comment on an important topic, another student interrupted him. The lengths some of his classmates went to see him fail disturbed him. Fortunately, Jake's professors saw this behavior and dealt with the jealousy by assigning Jake to a study group made up of his rivals. Soon after joining, the others realized that

Jake wasn't trying to show off, rather he wanted to liven up the class discussions by sharing insights he'd gained from a lifetime of reading. They came to respect his mind and his willingness to speak to them in French, and after a while, they decided maybe, they didn't mind this American as much as before.

The night before the wedding, Jake woke up feeling like an absolute wreck. He felt like he hadn't slept at all, worrying whether it would rain or if he had forgotten anything important. He wanted everything to be perfect for their wedding. He left his bed and stood, looking out over the moonlit courtyard and let his mind wander. Jake then sat at his desk and tried to do some research to clear his mind, but it was hopeless. The one thing he wasn't nervous about was marrying Manda. The promise of their lives together was the only thing keeping him from losing it completely. Jake thought of Manda, sleeping in her room in another wing of the chateaux and for the thousandth time, was thankful for her.

He walked over to the bathroom mirror, looked at himself, and prayed, "Please make me worthy of the love she gives me."

All at once, he felt a calm settle over him. *Bonne soirée mon amour,* Manda's voice said in his mind. *Today, we will become husband and wife. I love you now and always, and I can't wait to start our lives together. Don't worry. We have forgotten none of the arrangements and the wedding will be perfect. Now go back to sleep! You will need it today. Fais de beaux rêves my love.* He felt her soft lips kiss his temple and smiling he laid back in bed and fell into a restful sleep.

Manda was right. She always had a sense about these things. After a brief dawn shower that refreshed the gardens, the weather was perfect, and they forgot nothing. His parents were there along with a small group of family and close friends from home. When the doors opened to the chapel, the first sight Manda had was of Jake, tall and handsome in his tuxedo. *Oh! He even managed to get his hair combed!* She got a flutter in her chest, thinking of how much she loved this man. Jake would never forget how Amandine looked as her father walked her down the main aisle of the chapel. When they arrived at the alter, her father pulled back her veil, and Jake lost his breath. Her dark brown hair arranged on her bare shoulders, framing her face perfectly. Manda's face was serene and confident when she looked up at him. When he looked back into her eyes, his world stood still. Somewhere, in the distance, Jake heard Manda's voice, and he looked at her soft full lips forming his name. "Jacques… Jacques!!" Suddenly he snapped back to attention, hearing the chuckles of the small group in attendance. Red-faced, he grinned at Manda and said, "What are we waiting for?" and laughed along with the guests.

Chapter Thirteen

Preparations

When he came back from the meeting with the King, Jacques took Phillip and Amanda into the Great Room, closed the door, and sat in a chair lost in thought.

Finally, Phillip said, "Speak up, lad! Things cannot be as bad as all that!!"

Jacques glanced up at them saying, "Wait until you hear what the king has in mind, and then we will see." Amanda looked at Jacques and said, "Whatever it is my love, we will face it together!"

Jacques told them about his conversation with the king and his chancellor. To their credit, they took the news well. Phillip nodded his head as if he had expected this development, and he repeated the caution Gregory gave Jacques about keeping the news secret.

Amanda began to digest the news immediately. *Yes, I suspected this due to the Woodland Folk's treatment of Jacques after meeting him. It was with deference I'd never seen them give another human before. Even the Guardian was momentarily interested as Jacques passed by. I know, there will be many obstacles to his acceptance as king, even with those Houses that respect him. I sense half the Houses will not support him after the king dies, maybe even rebelling if the time is right. He does not fully appreciate how duplicitous the nobles can be, nor does he expect the traps they will set to embarrass him. Gregory, father, and I will have to prepare him.* Amanda realized she forgot to say, "Congratulations, my beloved! You will be one of the great kings of Aquitaine."

He stood and embraced her, saying, "Only if you are by my side." He kissed her forehead.

Lord Jacques felt he lived a double life. Along with meeting with Chancellor Gregory in secret, he made a public show of being involved in every detail of the wedding arrangements. Many citizens of Bordeaux smiled at the new bridegroom's extra attention to the wedding details, never suspecting his mind was elsewhere. Jacques had to digest all the Chancellor, Phillip, and Amanda taught him at night, as well as perform his duties as Lord of his House. It was, at times overwhelming, but through the patient instruction, he received Jacques managed his duties. Fortunately for Jacques the wedding plans were finalized due to Amanda's considerable organizational skills that she'd learned from her mother. Her time as the Lady of the House of Osprey had prepared her well.

When Jacques attended court with the rest of the nobles, he took care not to say anything to suggest he had received special instruction or favor. He listened to the petty squabbling of the others and wondered how anything ever got accomplished with all the gossip and backstabbing. He now understood the look on the king's face when the others on the council came to an impasse. The nobles weren't interested in solving problems as much as gaining some small measure of power and wealth the worst of these being Lucian of the House of Eagle. The next time he met with Gregory, Jacques talked about the steps needed in resetting the political game-board of the nobles. Gregory listened, gaining respect for how far the young lord had progressed in his lessons. However, as Chancellor, he thought it was good that the king was getting stronger because Jacques still had a lot to learn.

Finally, the time had come for Jacques to lay aside the affairs of state and devote himself fully to helping Amanda with the final wedding preparations. Despite his initial reluctance to be involved in the planning, Jacques found it refreshing to be doing something other than reading and thinking about ruling a kingdom. Most of all, he loved working with Amanda. He missed their easy banter and the way she teased him when his fingers were too big to do some delicate project.

She loved hearing him sing while he worked, and she would dance around the tables setting bowls in their place. Sometimes he would dance with her fast, spinning her all around the courtyard, and they would land dizzy in a pile of hay out of breath and laughing. As the morning wore on, birds would fly in and flit around Amanda's head, passing on congratulations from the Woodland Folk.

As their wedding day dawned, the early morning clouds gave way to beautiful blue skies. With the preparations set, all the bride and groom could do was wait for the bells to call the guests to the church (which to Phillip meant everybody). Jacques paced around the family chateaux, making sure all was perfect for Amanda's arrival. Her favorite flowers were gathered and set out, the rooms were spotless, and he made sure the servants stocked the kitchen with the wines and foods she liked best.

After surveying the grounds, and seeing that everything was ready, he turned to walk back inside as one of the king's men came riding through the open gates. He handed Jacques a folded note. Jacques looked at the king's seal impressed in thick red wax and broke it open. After reading the summons, he told the rider he would come at once.

As Jacques entered the throne room, the king's gray face and blue lips shocked him.

"Be not overly concerned on my appearance, Lord Jacques. I am not yet ready to join my fathers," he chuckled, starting a coughing fit. "I summoned you here to tell you that, within a month, you and Lady Amanda will move into the palace." Jacques started to protest, but he fell silent by the king's hand. "It is a matter of convenience, Lord Jacques. As Royal Chancellor, I require you be close by in case I need you. The staff is preparing comfortable quarters for you and your lady large enough to start a family," the king said with a smile. "Now go and give my congratulations to Lady Amanda as you begin your life as husband and wife!"

As Jacques rode through the gates of his chateaux, he was unsure of his feelings about the upcoming move. He looked around at the familiar setting and what surprised him was his reluctance to leave. Growing up, Jacques considered the Chateaux of the Lions to be just a place, but now he saw it as the only home he had ever known. He closed his eyes and remembered scenes from his childhood. His mother chasing him as a toddler around the courtyard, and playfully growling, holding her hands spread out like claws, while he trotted away on his tiny, chubby legs, squealing with delight. Jake saw his first time on a horse, and the day his father finally allowed him to pick a book from the library. Mostly, he saw scenes of his mother and father, and how they treated each other with love and respect. Most days were like a honeymoon for them, and Jacques hoped it would be the same as between him and Amanda.

Jacques smiled as he remembered the day he had introduced Amanda to his father. Leo had welcomed her into their home as an honored guest and member of the family.

Jacques thought of moments he used to sit with Leo and talk non-stop about Amanda's intelligence and good humor. How she saw things in a way he never did. Jacques told Leo about how much he enjoyed the long conversations with Amanda. He told his father of her innate connection with the world around her and how accomplished she was, and not only as Lady of the House.

Amanda was brilliant in her own right with her own ideas and opinions. Jacques spoke of how events in her past sometimes haunted her and how Amanda still struggled with her self-confidence, but she refused to let those things define who she was and how she lived her life, choosing to be loving, gracious, and forgiving.

As he thought of Amanda, Jacques was convinced that one thing that he respected most was her sense of right and wrong He smiled when he remembered those times she refused to stand by while others were treated badly. It was almost as if Amanda became another person as she faced down a bully or a cheat twice her size. It was comical as they flinched at her flashing eyes when she berated them in a low, almost growlly voice chasing after them as they scurried away.

Jacques recalled his last conversation with Leo concerning Amanda, sitting by the campfire on the night before the last battle. Jacques told Leo about Amanda's compassion for everyone she met and how she unconsciously drew others to her by her open spirit.

"I've never seen such compassion in anyone except Mother. That is one thing I love most about her," he said.

Leo looked at him with the smile he had only given to his wife and said, "Jacques, you love most everything about her! That was the same way I felt about your mother." Clapping Jacques on the back, Leo said with a catch in his throat, (something Jacques had never heard before.) "When we get back, I will talk to Phillip about you and Amanda and ask for his permission for you to court her." Just then, a servant interrupted his memories reminding him of the hour and his need to dress.

As Jacques and his men rode through the front gates of Lord Phillip's Chateaux, the Herald announced in a loud voice, "Royal Chancellor Jacques, Lord of the House of Lion." With every man dressed in his finest clothes and the Lion Coat of Arms embroidered on their chests, it was an impressive display. Amanda, hearing the commotion in the courtyard, peeked out the window and her knees shook a little when she saw Jacques sitting straight and proud on his horse.

She thought, *Soon, my love.*

Later, while standing at his place in the chapel's front, Jacques caught his first glimpse of Amanda as she walked down the aisle arm in arm with Phillip. His breath caught in his throat, and she walked towards him. She was tall, regal, and confident in her choice of a husband. He saw her smile from behind her veil, and his heart skipped a beat. Jacques thought he finally understood the full meaning of the word love and he knew there wasn't anything he wouldn't do to keep her happy and safe. As Phillip pulled back her veil, Amanda took her place next to him, for a moment Jacques became lost in her eyes. Jacques knew he would never forget how she looked at this moment or how he felt.

CHAPTER FOURTEEN

Years later, Jake still had trouble remembering the details of their wedding and the following reception. The only images he had in this mind were of Manda's smile and how gracefully she moved from table to table, greeting and talking to their guests. She treated every person as if they were the most important one there. Jake was always impressed by how she did that, but he also knew Manda had the ability to see a person more completely, understanding what was important to each one. Jake knew he'd had a wonderful time only because every wedding picture of him showed a delighted smile that he'd never seen before.

As time passed, Jake realized his life with Amandine and her ability to live each day to its fullest had an amazing effect on him. He saw the world around him in new and different ways, sometimes brighter and other times darker. She taught Jake to listen to the sounds of nature more deeply. He could now hear individual sounds and how they blended like an orchestra. Jake also noticed how Manda saw people differently and with a look or touch of their hand, could sense their moods, hurts, and joys. He brought her flowers just because he knew she'd like them. They would sometimes stop on the sidewalk to window shop and hold each other close. Many times, Jake and Manda attended local art and music festivals. Other times, she sat on his lap and poured out her feelings or told him about the events of the day. Jake loved the sound of Manda's voice. The best times were when they sat with his arms around her, oblivious to everything but each other.

Ever since Jake had met Manda, he recognized the things he loved and respected most about her were her mind, her beautifully free spirit, and the immeasurable depths of her heart. It never surprised him when strangers walked up to her on the street and spoke to her, acting as if they'd known her their whole life. Knowing she was born to be a healer of hearts and broken spirits, Jake came to accept this as a part of their life together. Sometimes, Jake would talk to Manda about a random topic just to watch her mind work at the speed of light. Sometimes, Jake would lay out a problem he wrestled with, and when he'd finished, she would find a core issue he had not fully thought through or had ignored. Other times he would talk about some obscure historical event he'd never come across before, and Manda would describe it in much greater detail than his research had produced.

When he asked her how she knew these things, she'd laugh and say, "Silly Jacques, I was there."

Jake had to admit their life together was wonderful, not that everything was perfect between them. They came from two very different cultures and languages, which often magnified how differently they saw things. Living together as husband and wife, they quickly learned to be less defensive and stubborn, and their life took on a rhythm of its own.

Two years later, Jake received his Master's Degree in history and was quickly hired as an assistant professor in history at the university. Manda was having great success as a professional photographer and makeup artist, gaining many clients all over Europe. In their spare time, they explored France and traveled to other countries. Manda and Jake shopped at the outdoor Farmer's Market on Saturdays and Sunday dinner was with the Auvergnes. They took long walks in the evenings, even when it rained or snowed. Jake and Manda grew closer and deeper in love every day, and Jake began to notice he had changed.

Over time, he had become more confident and self-assured when talking with colleagues and delivering lectures for students. Jake found his laugh came easier when before he would only smile. If they heard music playing during their walks, Jake would stop, bow, and take Amandine in his arms and dance with her on the sidewalk. Some of those people passing by would smile, others would frown, but Manda and Jake would laugh with delight. Jake found he was becoming more of the man he had always wanted to be, recognizing it was Manda's love and steadfast belief in him that gave him the confidence to live his life fully. It was this belief in his abilities that prompted Jake to begin a Ph.D. program in history at the university along with his teaching duties.

One morning, Manda woke Jake shaking him, saying, "Wake up sleepyhead, you will be late for class!" He quickly dressed and grabbed a piece of toast before heading for the door. As his hand touched the doorknob, he heard Amandine clear her throat, and smiling, he turned around giving her a sloppy goodbye kiss and bowing. "Je t'aime, Amandine," he said in a horrible French accent. Laughing, she swatted at him, saying, "Go to class, I have work to do too."

Later, Jake was in his office looking over the completed assignments of his students, when Dr. Gregory, the Chair of the University's History Department, walked in unexpectedly. Jake quickly stood up, causing the papers to fall on to the floor.

"Dr. Gregory," Jake said, "I'm sorry, did I miss an appointment with you?"

Stooping down to help pick the papers up, Dr. Gregory said, "No, Jacques, I was walking by and wanted to share some news with you. It's a beautiful day; let's take a stroll outside." As they walked along the path, Dr. Gregory asked about Amandine and how Jake was enjoying married life.

Then Dr. Gregory said, "Jacques, several of us in the department have been watching your work and the way the students are responding to you, and we are pleased by what we've seen and by how you've become more confident. Also, we are impressed by the scholarship of your published papers. You have been doing excellent work, and it won't be long before you earn your Ph.D. This is all to say, we have been so impressed with you, the decision is unanimous in promoting you to a full professor of history. It will take effect with the new term."

Surprised, Jake said, "Dr. Gregory, I… I don't know what to say."

"Just say yes, then you and I will celebrate with a glass of wine in my office!"

Jake told him yes, shook his hand, and followed Dr. Gregory to his office. There, he heard Dr. Gregory describe the extra duties this new position had but also all the benefits, including a pay raise. Jake couldn't wait to get home to tell Amandine the big news!

That night, Jake practically ran home. He had already made plans for what they could do with the added income. He took the stairs two at a time and was out of breath when he burst in the door.

He called out, "Amandine! Wait until you hear my news! I can't wait to tell you that…"

Manda interrupted him by saying, "We're going to have a baby!"

Chapter Fifteen

Growing and Stretching

After the wedding ceremony, Jacques took Amanda aside to a quiet place and quickly shared the news about their move into the Royal Palace.

She smiled up at him saying, "It was going to happen eventually, so I'm glad it happened sooner! I don't care where we live, my beloved, as long as it's with you."

They kissed again and joined their guests. Jacques marveled at her apparent ease as she moved among the tables and greeted their guests, especially since she preferred more intimate gatherings rather than celebrations that involved the whole city.

I am the most fortunate man who has ever lived! he thought. After all the toasts and the meals came many vows of loyalty to the Houses of Lion and Osprey. Later, all the guests cheered, serenading the young couple as they left to spend their first night together as husband and wife.

A week after the wedding, Jacques wondered how many newly married couples spent their first month of marriage together, moving their belongings to a new home.

After seeing their new palace home, Amanda thought, *The king did not disappoint. His choice of an apartment for us is perfect.* The rooms were spacious and warm, with a fireplace in every chamber. The windows let in plenty of sunlight and looked out over the ancient forest where they loved to roam.

Chancellor Gregory took great care in choosing their furniture, ensuring it was of the highest quality and worthy of a person of Lord Jacques's stature. He even had their bedchamber decorated in blues and greens, the colors of both their Houses. *I must be sure to thank the chancellor for his kindness and attention to detail,* she thought.

Even though Jacques was gone a good deal, learning his new responsibilities as Royal Chancellor, he spent every free moment he had with Amanda. They still rode out to the forest to see their friends and to keep up on the news of the Woodland Folk. When they were alone in their private chambers, Jacques would sometimes sing, sweeping her up in his strong arms and dancing with her, causing her to cry with laughter. In the evenings, Amanda taught Jacques a more comprehensive way to play chess, one in which he would see the whole chess board instead of only his next move. By learning to be patient and using a more subtle strategy, he ceased applying his more aggressive style. This skill would be important in future battles, both real and political. He may not have won all the games with Amanda, but at least he won some.

Often, they would spend their evenings in quiet conversation, laughing or discussing new and interesting things one or both had read about and wanted to share. Jacques loved listening to the sound of Amanda's voice. She often complained about her squeaky voice, but Jacques found it to be rich, almost musical in tone He especially loved to listen to the sound of her laughter. These were the most precious times they shared because they truly enjoyed talking with each other and would often laugh and talk until dawn. Sometimes, their conversations became heated and turned into arguments. In those times, Jacques was stubborn, and Amanda could be blunt, verging on being sarcastic. Though, over time, they both came to rely on each other's experience and wisdom, vowing to forgive each other quickly and never go to bed angry, at least most times.

Over the next three years, Jacques learned the ways of the royal court and its politics. He learned to see and avoid the traps some disenchanted nobles had laid for him. Quietly, to honor a promise he made to himself long ago, Jacques arranged for a tutor to fill the gaps in Amanda's formal education. As her knowledge over a wide range of topics increased, Jacques developed an even deeper respect for Amanda's ability to solve problems for which he had little time to resolve.

Soon, Jacques realized he had not been as involved with the duties of the House of Lion as he needed to be, and he asked Amanda to take control over the more important tasks, teaching staff and servants to do the rest. In doing so, the other members of the House came to know and love their new lady, recognizing her position in the House. As the former Lady of the House of Osprey, Amanda was well qualified to show them the intricacies of running a House and providing the staff with the needed direction in maintaining the House's business ventures.

The other Houses and the Court considered the change scandalous. The gossips said, "The Lord of the House is handing over his duties and responsibilities to a woman?"

"Has the Lion lost his senses? Everyone knows women are irrational and prone to emotional outbursts!"

Of course, none of the lords of the other Houses noticed how much responsibility they had left to the ladies of their Houses. The lords were often unwilling or (more often) incapable of dealing with the day-to-day management of their Houses. The lords preferred to ride and hunt, which left little time to bother with reading, mathematics, or the sciences. Soon, though, even the most hard-headed skeptics had to admit that Amanda excelled as the House's business interests became more profitable, and the farms were more productive than others in the kingdom. The House of Lion quickly became one of the most highly regarded of the noble families. Some of the Houses even sent their foremen to Amanda in secret to learn how to flourish the way the House of Lion did.

Later that year, Jacques slept past his normal time. He was exhausted from the king relegating many of the royal duties to him. Amanda sat on the bed next to him and said, "Wake up, sleepyhead! We have things to do today."

Jacques groaned and rolled over, putting a pillow over his head. "Just a little longer, Amanda!" At that moment, he heard an urgent pounding on their chamber door, and he sat up in bed.

Throwing on a robe, Amanda opened the door and saw Chancellor Gregory standing there looking pale.

"Lord Jacques, you must come now! The king is dying.

CHAPTER SIXTEEN

"We're going to have what?" Jake asked.

"Un bébé, mon amour," Manda said smiling.

"We're going to have a baby!" Jake said as he picked her up and spun around their small living room. *This day keeps getting better and better,* he thought and then kissed her half a dozen times.

He sat on the couch, and she sat in his lap saying, "Now it's your turn to tell me your news, Jacques."

He told her the details of his promotion. They were overjoyed by the abundance of good news. When they called their parents, they had to set the phone on the table because the shouts of joy and congratulations were so loud.

However, once the news about the baby sunk in, Jake and Manda realized their once very spacious and romantic apartment was barely big enough for two. It would never fit three along with everything else that came with having a newborn. They soon discovered even with Jake's increase in pay, finding a large enough apartment would be too expensive.

When they talked about it with Manda's parents over dinner, her father said, "Why not move in here? The chateaux is much too big for just your mother and me. You could have your own wing, and that would give you plenty of room not only for you and the baby but also for a photography studio and office. Plus, the university is closer to us than your apartment. Besides, all of this will be yours someday."

Manda looked at Jake across the table, and he slowly nodded back, and with tears in her eyes, she said, "Merci papa et maman. Your offer is an answer to a prayer."

"Then it settled!" Looking at his wife, he took her hand and said, "We will once again have a little one in the house." In raising his glass, he toasted the occasion.

After moving into the family chateaux, Amandine and Jake discovered their life hadn't changed all that much. They still went to work every day, and even with Jake's new duties, he still made it home around the same time. The two of them still took long walks in the soft evenings and sometimes danced in the moonlit street to music playing from open windows. On weekends, Jake and Manda still sipped coffee with friends at sidewalk cafes, and since she couldn't travel as much with the pregnancy, Manda produced a series of very popular photos on the wild roses covering the old city walls. They shopped and made dinner together. Manda still sat on Jake's lap as they quietly talked. As the pregnancy progressed, Amandine was secretly happy she didn't have to climb the stairs to their old apartment or try to navigate around the small space, especially after the doctor confirmed what she already knew. She would have twins. Jake recognized neither of them knew much about taking care of babies and was happy to have Manda's mother nearby.

Jake also tried to do more around the house as the due date approached. He tried to copy what he saw Amandine do a thousand times, and he never quite got it right with the laundry and cleaning. However, this was especially true with his cooking. He would forget some ingredients or skip a step in the recipe. Once he wanted to surprise her by baking her favorite cake. He bought two boxes of cake mix, one for each layer. He mixed the batter and poured it into the cake pans. Later, when he looked in the oven, he discovered the batter had baked into what looked like two giant mushrooms! Only then did he read the instructions on the box and see he'd only needed one box for a two-layer cake.

Manda walked into the kitchen just as he was taking the pans from the oven. Jake said, "Surprise, we have cake!" and both of them dissolved into laughter.

Early one evening close to Manda's due date, Jake was making tea for her when she told him she was felt uncomfortable and they should go to the hospital.

"Just to be sure," she said.

Later that night at around 1:11 am, their son Gerard was born, followed by his sister Amélie at 2:22 am. As soon as the nurse told Jake he was a father, he sat down and missed the chair, winding up on the floor. When Manda's father stopped laughing, he helped Jake up and congratulated him as he pumped Jake's hand up and down.

"Twins! Life is good, son!"

Jake stood in the doorway of her room and silently gazed at Manda. She looked beautiful and tired, and he knew he had never loved her more than in that moment.

Looking over at his smiling face, she whispered, "Come in and meet your children."

Jake slowly walked to her and kissed her, saying, "Manda my love. How are you feeling?"

"I'm fine. Just a little tired." Patting the bed next to her, she said, "Come, mon amor and sit by me." As Jake sat on the edge of her bed, the nurse placed a baby in each one of Jake's arms. Amandine sat forward, wrapping her arms around Jake and putting her chin on his shoulder.

She asked, "So, beloved, what do you think?"

Jake answered, "They are as beautiful as their mother. So which is which?" Laughing, Amandine playfully punched his shoulder.

Jake's parents were on the first plane to France and hurried to the hospital to see their grandchildren and Manda and Jake. The Auvergne's gracefully invited them to stay at the chateaux for as long as they needed. As Jake got home later that evening, he walked to the great room to see the two grandmothers hugging and wiping tears. The two grandfathers slapped each other on their backs and congratulated each other. Upon seeing Jake walk in, the grandparents embraced him in a weepy, group hug. It was then Jake saw two empty bottles of strong port wine and four half-filled glasses. Smiling to himself, he thought it explained a lot.

Over the next two months, the love that only grandmothers can provide surrounded the new family. He often received unprompted, "sage" grandfatherly advice. After Jake's parents returned home, life became less noisy but more hectic. It was hard to imagine what life could be like as parents of twins. However, with Manda's parents help along with regular visits to America to see Jake's parents, the young family thrived. Over the next few years, life flew by. With Jake's studies completed, he was now a Doctor of History. Manda was much sought after as a photographer, makeup artist, and a fashion model. She had a stellar reputation for her work on both sides of the camera. Gerard and Amélie grew into small versions of Manda with her dark hair and green eyes. He noticed how gentle pets and other animals were around them. In looking over his life, his family, and work, Jake couldn't remember a time when he had been happier.

Chapter Seventeen

A Heavy Crown

acques hurried after the chancellor to the king's bed chambers, dreading what he would find. Gregory softly knocked and entered without waiting for an answer. Jacques looked at his king lying on his bed, wheezing and gasping for each breath. Bright and warm sunlight from the window poured over the king, but he still needed blankets to keep from shivering. Seeing Jacques, the king waved him over to the bed. Jacques leaned over with his ear close to the king's mouth listening for Louis' final words.

"Lord Jacques, tonight I will be greeted by my Fathers, and I hope they will be satisfied with my reign." He paused, trying to suck in the air he needed but could no longer receive. "Time is short so listen well…"

For the next half an hour, the king told Jacques the latest state secrets, the court intrigues, and the impending problems he would face with the various Noble Houses.

"Gregory has told me you have been a quick study, and you are well prepared to take my place on the Throne of Aquitaine. I urge you to be cautious and to watch for the nobles' plots. Half of them dislike you and are suspicious of you." Another pause, more wheezing… "Make your changes slowly and…" Louis' eyes got big as he tried to suck in air, "…listen to Gregory. He is by far the wisest man in the kingdom. Also, listen to your wife, Lady Amanda! She is wise as well. I foresee she will be a blessing to you and Aquitaine. She will be your most loyal ally and will help you build a new and glorious future for our people! A future we cannot even imagine. Lord Jacques, I name you Regent of the Kingdom to reign until your coronation. Rule well and wisely. Long live the king!" The king's energy spent, Louis fell back into his bed, gasping, his lips turning a deep blue, and he lapsed into a coma.

Chancellor Gregory bowed his head and took a deep breath. "We must call the Royal Advisors, the Royal Counsellors, and the Heads of the Nobel Houses together. We must begin the Death Watch."

Later that evening, surrounded by the Heads of the Noble Houses, King Louis passed from this earth and was warmly welcomed by his fathers and ancestors. After his court witnessed and certified the king's death, Chancellor Gregory produced a scroll sealed with the Royal Seal stamped into the thick red wax, and he showed the unbroken seal to all those gathered.

As Gregory broke the wax seal, Jacques felt the anticipation and the hunger for power in the small room. Then the chancellor made a show of opening the document and allowed the Court to review it. Few except Jacques and Gregory could read it, but all the nobles recognized the king's signature certifying its authenticity. Taking a deep breath, Chancellor Gregory read King Louis' edict naming the Royal Chancellor Jacques, Lord of the House of Lion, Aquitaine's Regent and Heir to the throne. Jacques watched impassively as the faces of some nobles showed confusion while other's looks of anticipation turned to shock and controlled anger. Lord Lucian betrayed nothing. He was already plotting his next moves.

The dead king lay in state for seven days at the front of the Cathedral. He was protected around the clock by an honor guard of his most loyal knights. His simple wooden casket was covered with the Royal Standard of Aquitaine, while a procession of the king's Royal Court led by the Regent of Aquitaine passed by to give their final respects to the king. Later, thousands of mourners did the same, lighting candles to symbolize the prayers they said to ease Louis' passing into eternity. Over these seven days, the Bishop said three Holy Masses for King Louis, and many feasts were given in his honor before they laid him to rest in the Royal Tomb under the alter.

As the people gathered to honor their late king, some of the most powerful men in the Kingdom met in secret to destroy all that he had built. Five nobles were seated at a round table in the private chambers of Lord Bernard of the House of Bear. Joining him was Lord Chevelle of the House of Fox, Lord Henri of the House of Panther, Lord Lucian of the House of Eagle, and Lord Percival of the House of Mouflon. At the head of the table sat Lucian. Outwardly, he was tall, handsome, charismatic, athletic, and used to being the center of attention. He had a predator's sense of just how to act to put others at ease. Then, once he gained their trust, he would betray them and take advantage of them. Lucian cared only for meeting his own needs, most often at the expense of others.

Reluctantly he brought his attention back to the blowhard who was shouting, "NO! NO, I SAY." Bernard slammed his massive hairy fist on the table, making the cups jump. "I will not abide this…this upstart to take my rightful place on the throne!"

The other nobles glanced at each other, not at all liking the assumption that Bernard would be the next king, but they let him blow himself out.

"Louis must have gone senile to expect us to bow and scrape to this young pup!"

"Calm yourself, Bernard," said the soft, silky voice of Lucian. "He has not been crowned yet, and even if he is, so what? The young Lion cannot accomplish anything without the support of the Houses. We have the power, and we will bend him to our will."

"I am not so sure, Lucian," said Henri. "Jacques is popular among the people and the other Houses. Truthfully, I have never seen him bow to anyone's will."

Lucian chuckled in a whispery sound, not unlike that of a knife edge being sharpened on a stone. "Ah Henri, what does the truth have to do with anything?"

As the three-month mourning period for King Louis ended, the preparations for the coronation of the new King of Aquitaine neared completion. As Regent, Jacques had done well in overseeing the Kingdom due to the intensive training he had received from Chancellor Gregory, Phillip, and Amanda. The Heads of the Houses of Osprey, Wolf, Lynx, and Badger were impressed and prepared their oaths of loyalty to their new king.

The Houses of Bear, Fox, Panther, Eagle, and Mouflon were unhappy about how easily the upstart had sidestepped the political traps. They had planned to show how badly unprepared Jacques was to be crowned king. At their last meeting, they had reluctantly agreed to swear an oath of loyalty but continued to look for ways to unseat the young Lion. Before adjourning the meeting, they agreed to name themselves the "Steadfast Houses" to distinguish themselves as the nobles who rejected any change, holding fast to the traditions and customs of Aquitaine.

At least until it becomes… inconvenient, Lucian thought, laughing to himself.

Behind the scenes of the Royal Court, Jacques had meetings with the advisors who Gregory trusted the most. The subject most hotly debated was Lady Amanda's role as the wife of the king. Jacques stated that Amanda should be crowned queen during the coronation ceremony and serve alongside him on the throne. The advisors had a much different role in mind for her. Some said she should simply be the king's consort or wife and mother to the royal heirs. Others felt she could use her considerable talents in managing the palace staff and lady's in waiting. While still others thought she could organize the efforts to care for the widows, orphans, and needy, all things that are feminine showing Aquitaine what a fine choice the king had made for a wife.

Jacques was adamant, however, saying any role other than queen would not allow her to serve Aquitaine to the fullest extent, to which Gregory agreed. The last warning the advisors gave before they agreed to the king's demand was, a woman having equal stature to the king would unnerve the population and the Noble Houses.

Jacques said, "Those people finally accepted it when Amanda became my co-head of my House, they'll accept her as queen. My decision is final."

As the last of the advisors left the room, shaking their heads, Gregory said, "You know Sire, they are not wrong about this. Both you and Lady Amanda will have to convince people of just how worthy she is. Only then, will they come to accept and love Amanda as their rightful queen."

As the eventful day arrived, it seemed to Jacques and Amanda that the entire kingdom had gathered for the Coronation Ceremony. The people crowded the procession route from early in the day, claiming their spot to watch the procession. The excitement and anticipation grew as the time drew closer for the procession to pass, with people jockeying with one another for the best view. Was Jacques as handsome and tall as people said? Was Amanda the extraordinary beauty she was rumored to be? As the trumpets rang out, all conversation stopped as all eyes turned to the street.

Slowly, Jacques rode along the cobblestone avenue leading to the cathedral, dressed in royal robes of Aquitaine. To his right rode Amanda, sidesaddle on her horse, dressed in much the same way. At first, the people stared at the attractive couple sitting straight and proud on their prancing horses. Amanda and Jacques heard the murmurs of approval amid the cheers, and they smiled at each other. Still, the onlookers noticed that the lady was riding a horse instead of traveling in a coach as the king's consorts had in the past, and they wondered to each other what it meant. As the Steadfast Nobles rode by, they also heard the whispers of the crowd concerning Lady Amanda, and they smiled at each other, thinking this is their opportunity to drive a wedge between the people and the king as he began his reign.

Jacques and Amanda arrived at the cathedral and were formally greeted by a solemn bishop. Leading them up red-carpeted stairs, and into the dark narthex, they waited for the rest of the nobles to process into the sanctuary. Jacques gazed into the cavernous space, noticing how the light came through the large stained-glass windows, sending columns of colored light pooling on the flagstones. He smelled the softened bee's wax of lit candles and the sandalwood incense the acolytes dispersed in white clouds by swinging their golden sensors on golden chains.

When all was ready, Jacques and Amanda led the procession up the wide aisle to the raised dais where two thrones awaited them. Everyone who saw them remarked how both Jacques and Amanda looked regal as they confidently walked towards their future place in history. With their cloaks removed, the guests had their first look at the couple's royal clothing. Jacques' clothes were simple: A deep blue tunic and leggings with riding boots polished to a deep gloss. They embroidered his tunic with a simple design in silver thread. As Amanda passed, however, there were soft gasps as they marveled at her brilliant, form-fitting white dress shimmering from subtle vines embroidered with metallic green floss, topped with blossoms stitched from a gold thread that captured and reflected the light. The flowers appeared to wave in an unseen wind as she walked down the aisle.

As the nobles, the lords and ladies, royal guests from the surrounding kingdoms, and their various entourages took their seats in the Sanctuary, they wondered why there were two thrones. The ceremony began with Jacques and Amanda kneeling on cushions at the bottom of the stairs. Choirs sang hymns, and the bishop led them in responsive psalms. At the appointed time, the bishop recited prayers and called down blessings on the two young monarchs, finishing by saying the ancient words of the sacred rite of succession. Then Jacques and Amanda, hand-n-hand, climbed the stairs to the dais, turned and faced the guests, and sat upon the thrones. They were anointed with holy oil; and crowned king and queen.

When the ceremony ended, the bishop turned to the audience and said in a loud voice, the declaration of loyalty, "The king is dead! Long live the king! Long live the queen!" The assembled guests; repeated the declaration. The Steadfast Houses, did not swear allegiance to the queen.

CHAPTER EIGHTEEN

As they celebrated their tenth anniversary, Jake couldn't have been happier. Life with Manda, Gerard, and Amélie was magical. He was now the head of the university's History Department. Manda's modeling career and photography studio were thriving. Best of all, the children were blossoming into amazing human beings. The family would live for ten months in France and two months in America with Jake's parents. That is, when his parents weren't visiting, which they often did.

Everything was perfect until Manda began to have occasional migraines. Neither of them thought much about it, assuming it was stress related. Over time, though the headaches grew more frequent and sometimes the pain was so severe Manda would spend the day in bed. Jake took Manda to various doctors who performed test after test, and they all arrived at the same conclusion, Amandine had a brain tumor. They had no explanation of why or knew of any effective treatment other than chemo or radiation. A surgeon suggested an operation but couldn't guarantee a complete recovery. The doctors prescribed medication to ease the symptoms but warned her these things were not a cure, and they needed to seek a more aggressive solution. Manda nodded her head, took medicine, and the pain subsided for a while. Time and time again, Jake would encourage her to see a specialist, even offering to take her to America for a consultation, but Manda would always change the subject.

Within six months, it was clear even to Jake's untrained eye, Amandine was getting worse, and he tried everything he could to get her to seek a more aggressive treatment. Jake pleaded, cried, yelled, argued, used guilt, and even had her parents talk with her. Still, nothing would move her to change her mind. Once, Gerard and Amélie spoke to her about it, and afterward, they told Jake they understood their mother's reasons and wouldn't push her anymore. Defeated, Jake made whatever time they had left the most magical yet.

The little family spent hours in the chateaux's gardens where the butterflies would collect on Manda's head like a crown, making them all laugh as Jake gave Manda a freshly cut long-stemmed rose to use as a royal scepter. She gave royal proclamations to the family, and they bowed to Queen Amandine. Jake would take her on their nightly strolls through their neighborhood in her wheelchair, and when he heard the music, he would wheel the chair around, dancing with her as she laughed with delight. The family spent every Saturday at the Farmer's Market and every Sunday with her parents. Those days when Manda felt up to it, Jake pushed her on the trails of the ancient forest near the chateaux where the animals ran up and chattered or sang or yipped to her and Manda would smile and talk back to them.

One evening during their nightly conversation, Amandine was curled up on Jake's lap wrapped in a blanket. She said, "Mon amour, I know you don't understand or accept my decision about not seeking treatment. You love me and want us to grow old together. I want that too, but you have forgotten mine is an ancient soul, as is yours. I had told this to you when we first met, but perhaps you didn't fully understand what this means. It doesn't mean I don't love you or the children. I love all of you with everything that I am, and if it were up to me, I'd stay with you forever. However, it isn't up to me. I realize I have accomplished what I was put on Earth to do, and it is now time to go home."

Hot tears coursed down Jake's face, and he asked bitterly, "And what was that?"

"To love you, of course. To love you and to give the world amazing children who will accomplish amazing things. During my time here, I was to heal the hurts of the people I met and stand up to injustice. I was to show the world a better way to live and love. Last, I was to give you the confidence to live your life fully. Because of this, you too will change and improve the lives of thousands of people."

She looked up at him and kissed him. "Don't be sad for me, my darling. I am not leaving you completely. I will live on through our children, and I will always be close by you. Oh, mon amour, I don't have the words to tell you how incredible it is to be loved so completely and unconditionally by you and to have had the privilege to give it back to you." Taking his face in her hands, she kissed his closed eyes, tasting his tears. She said, "Please let me go with your full heart, Jacques. I promise we will be together again. Our love for each other is eternal. It is the only thing we take with us when we leave this world, and I will never let yours go."

As the seasons changed, so did Manda. She grew weak and frail, and Jake sat with her in his lap by the window as the sun washed over them. On warm days, he would open the window so Manda could hear the birds singing and sometimes the birds would land on the sill giving her a private concert. Other times it sounded as if the forest played its own music for her. Manda would close her eyes and smile as her pain eased for a while. Finally, the family gathered together in the garden one warm summer day. The flowers were in full bloom and the birds were singing to her. Jake held her, as always, on his lap softly singing her favorite song while gently stroking her hair.

Amandine looked into Jake's eyes and said, "Mon amour, I will love you forever, and I will see you again." With a serene smile, she passed from the Earth. The birds and insects stopped their singing for a moment to honor their friend's passing.

Jake buried his face in her hair and whispered, "No…don't go. Don't go anywhere without me."

Amandine's funeral was as beautiful as she was. Family and friends from all walks of life gathered from across Europe and America to remember her and to honor her life. Jake wasn't surprised to hear how everyone had a story to share about how Amandine touched their life or how she shared a kindness that changed the direction of their life. Manda still drew people to her and healed them even now. If it was possible to measure the value of a person's life by the love and laughter shared at their funeral, then Manda's life was incalculable. Jake greeted everyone and politely listened to their memories of Manda. He laughed when appropriate and comforted when needed. As they lowered her coffin into her grave, the light went out of his world. He looked over at the gravestones next to her's and asked Lord Phillip and Lady Rachel to take care of his beloved.

The next months were nothing but pain for Jake. Everywhere he went, and everything he saw reminded him of Manda. He stopped going to the Market and taking evening walks because those were things he did with her. He turned down dinners with friends because he couldn't bear the sad looks and kindness they gave him. Every time Jake closed his eyes, he saw her face. He watched family films, so he could hear her voice again, even though it ripped through him every time he did. Jake took a leave of absence from the University, and he only left the chateaux when necessary.

Manda's mother took charge of the twins and cared for Jake like he was a sick child. She cleaned their rooms, cooked their meals, did their laundry, and listened to him as he carried on conversations with her daughter as if she was in the room with him. She had never seen pain as sharp as Jake's and in desperation, she called his mother to come and take him home for a while. Jake needed to be in a place where he didn't see Manda every waking moment.

Jake's mother fought back the tears when she first saw her son. He had lost so much weight that his clothes hung on his frame. His blue-gray eyes were listless, and his hair hadn't seen a brush in weeks. Manda's mom told her the only time Jake showed any life at all was when he was around Gerard and Amélie. It was a quiet plane ride back to America and his parent's house. Pain radiated off him in waves. Jake would give one-word answers to any question they asked. Once in the house, he sat alone in his room, looking at a picture of himself and Manda from college. His mom thought, if he would just cry, he could get it over with once and for all, but the tears wouldn't come. One day, Jake noticed the scent of Manda's favorite perfume and felt her lips as she kissed his cheek. Then, all at once, Jake started to cry and cry and cry. He cried until he fell into an exhausted sleep.

When he woke up, Jake felt something warm and familiar under his hand. Picking it up, he saw it was his old book, *I didn't pack this.*

Just then, he heard Manda's voice.

No, you didn't, my love. I asked Gerard to pack it because it is there where you will find me. Don't be sad for me. I am free from pain now. Please, dearest, for my sake and those of our children, live! Our Gerard and Amélie need you to be present in their lives, and your students need your knowledge. Our parents need their son, and the world needs amazing men like you. The world and the people who live in it need the kind of unconditional love you live out day after day.

Jacques, you've put yourself back in that safe bubble where I first found you. You need to find the courage to once again break out of it and fully live your life. You are the finest man, husband, father, teacher, and friend I've ever known. The world needs you to be all those things. Stop mourning a wife whose love and devotion to you will never die and who is with you whenever you need her. You and your love were the greatest gifts in my life, and they live on still. Now sleep and wake up ready to face the world again. One last thing, mon amour, write your book. The world needs to hear from you! Have no fear, beloved. We will be together again.

That night, Jake didn't dread going to sleep.

When he woke, Jake found his mom and dad in the kitchen. His mom saw a different man from the one she brought home. This Jake was rested, relaxed, smiling, and ready to talk. He spent the next month under his mother's care. She made sure he ate, talked, and exercised by walking with her through the woods. Jake kept his promise and started writing the first of the many books he would write throughout his life. He wrote about his angel, Manda, telling her story so the world would know there were still amazing and beautifully magical people living in the world.

He spoke with the twins and the Auvergne's by telephone, who were overjoyed to hear the change in his voice. By the time he arrived back at the chateaux, he had gained weight and smiled more. He was still sad and missed Amandine terribly, but every time he sighed, calling out her name, he smelled her perfume and felt an ethereal embrace that made him forget his loneliness for a while. When Jake experienced one problem or another, his angel was there to advise and protect. When students would disrespect him in the back of the class, somehow their keys or homework would mysteriously go missing. Those times when Jake had trouble making a difficult decision regarding the twins or in life, he would hear a soft whisper giving a gentle and wise suggestion that always turned out to be right. However, in the dark and lonely times, Jacques would reread the magical book and find her as Amanda, just as Manda promised.

Chapter Nineteen

Fracturing

The weeks and months following his coronation were frustrating for the new King. Every meeting with his advisors brought either a new problem or a new wrinkle in an old, solved problem. There were constant questions about the queen and her duties. Was she to serve in equal capacity? If so, how would it work if they disagreed about some important issue? Also, his days were filled with an endless list of legal issues, tax issues, land use issues, diplomatic questions, and a never-ending and long overdue barrage of day-to-day decisions he could not delegate. The most frustrating distraction was the split in the Noble Houses. It became clear early on that five of the Houses supported the king's proposals and five who were always finding fault with the smallest nuances, leading to what seemed like endless debates about urgent problems. It was almost as if they had conspired to weaken his reputation with the people.

After the latest meeting ended, King Jacques and Chancellor Gregory were alone in the council chambers.

The king shook his head, saying, "Now I understand why Louis was always in a foul mood." Looking at his chancellor, he asked, "How do you think the people are accepting Queen Amanda? How much longer do I have to wait before she can join me in these meetings?"

The question was a continuation of a larger conversation. King Jacques wanted Queen Amanda to have a greater role in ruling the kingdom. Chancellor Gregory agreed but also cautioned patience.

"You know the old saying, Sire. Petit à petit, l'oiseau construit son nid. Little by little, the bird builds its nest. Be patient, even with our small actions, we are getting closer to your goal. Allow the people to warm to the idea of a queen. Then, bring her into the meetings and slowly give her increasingly more responsibility." The chancellor said, "The queen is doing well and gaining the support of the minor Houses and the common folk. The truth is, Sire, she is respected and well loved. Unfortunately, I have heard rumors you are the one they are dissatisfied with."

The king slowly nodded his head, saying, "With good reason, Gregory. I have given the people nothing but deferrals for long-needed improvements and delays in making the simplest decisions."

"Yes, Sire. I am afraid the division between the Nobles is having a far-reaching ripple effect. The people do not blame the Heads of the Houses. They blame you, fearing your youth and inexperience are the problems. I am afraid if we bring the queen in now, the perception will be you are weak and indecisive, showing you need to rely on Queen Amanda to accomplish anything."

The king sighed and said, "I understand."

Then frowning, the way he always did when wrestling with a difficult problem, the king said, "Is there a way to include her as an advisor? To sit in the meetings without taking part but give us her council in private."

Gregory shook his head, saying, "I am afraid that is a rather inelegant solution, Sire. The five nobles would see through your plan and be even more obstinate, creating added roadblocks. However, perhaps there is a way to be less obvious about involving the queen. Some years ago, I discovered a niche behind the tapestry of the 'Maid and the Unicorn.' None of the current nobles know it is there. The queen could sit there in secret and listen, accomplishing the same thing. However, no one besides us can know she is there. If discovered, it would cause great harm to your relationship with even the loyal Houses."

That night, Jacques and Amanda discussed the plan. She was equally frustrated by her lack of involvement. Amanda loved her role as healer of minds, hearts, and the souls of those she encountered daily, and the people loved her for it. However, she was also one who sought solutions to problems plaguing the kingdom, and she desperately wanted to serve her people better. She reluctantly agreed to the plan, telling Jacques how undignified it was to hide behind a tapestry, but Amanda knew he would not ask this of her if it was not important.

The next day, Queen Amanda arrived an hour before the Nobles and found the niche furnished with a comfortable chair and table with a goblet of water ready for her. The space was small, dark, and dusty, but she would manage. As she settled in, beginning to collect her thoughts, she heard the door to the Council Chamber open and two sets of footsteps entered the room. She immediately felt sick to her stomach in the way she always did when near people with evil souls or intentions.

"Are you sure no one saw us?" said a gruff voice she recognized as Lord Bernard.

"Calm yourself, no one saw us, and no one will hear us," said another, smoother voice that Amanda knew to be Lord Lucian. "Our conversation will be as private as ever."

And with that, the lords went on at length to discuss how to block the king's latest plan on improving schools and educating the common people. Amanda felt the waves of animosity these lords held for her and the king. The feelings were so strong she felt slightly light-headed.

If this is what I'm feeling with just these two, how will I manage with all five?

With some effort, the queen composed herself long enough to push through the nausea and focus on the discussion.

Later, when sitting with the king and Chancellor Gregory, the queen told all that she had heard and sensed. In finishing her report, she said, "The ultimate goal is to destroy us and end our reign, my husband. I learned they call themselves the Steadfast Nobles and plan to unseat you as king. Lord Bernard sees himself as taking your place, but I sense Lord Lucian is the one behind this and will claim the throne for himself."

Gregory nodded his head. "That makes sense my queen. Before King Louis made King Jacques his heir, Lucian was first among the nobles in succession to the throne. He had the most to lose in this. Lucian always had a lust for power, a black heart and a blacker soul." Looking at the king, he said, "As I recall, he was one of your chief tormentors while growing up and rivaled for the hand of the queen. It must gall him to bow to you."

As Jacques listened, he became still and thoughtful. Finally, he said, "I am sorry, dearest, to have put you in that situation. I know how such people affect you. It must have been exhausting for you, especially in that little space."

Amanda stood and walked over to her husband, took his hand, and smiled up at him. "Thank you for that, my love, but it was worth the discomfort to discover who is behind this. Perhaps now we can think of a way to thwart their plots before they cause any more harm."

Over the next month, the king, queen, and chancellor laid out future plans to avoid the traps of the Steadfast Nobles, using those same methods against them. Over time, the influence of the Steadfast faded enough to include the queen more and more in the royal affairs of the kingdom, including being present at meetings with his advisors who welcomed her (and the Steadfast Nobles who did not.)

As the king and queen became more confident in their duties, the kingdom began to thrive. New schools were built, theatres opened to new playwrights, books were published in greater numbers, crops increased, science and philosophy advanced, and the people felt a renewed sense of hope. There was talk of a new renaissance for Aquitaine. However, this newfound prosperity attracted the attention of the rebel leader, Morlok of the Ignominia. Since the defeat of their rebellion some years ago, Morlok had slowly recruited the disgraced men from the countryside and surrounding kingdoms, building an even greater rebel army. Morlok's hunger for revenge and power grew alongside his army.

Over time, Morlok sent his spies into Aquitaine, to discover the power of Aquitaine army's; and uncover any weakness and frustration among the people, hoping to use it to his advantage. As his spies returned, most spoke of a strong army and the people of Aquitaine being optimistic. One spy, however, told of a group named the Steadfast Nobles who were made up of half the Noble Houses. They were very dissatisfied with the young king. After hearing this news, Morlok set a plan into motion.

Over the next year, Morlok sent emissaries in secret to meet with Lucian, Morlok recognized Lucian's excessive vanity and overall lack of scruples made him ripe for manipulation. Morlok offered Aquitaine and her queen as a fiefdom to Lucian if he would convince the other Houses to not defend Aquitaine from any attack the Ignominia may or may not make on the kingdom. Lucian's eyes glittered in anticipation of that day. He would unseat the upstart and sit on the throne, keeping Amanda at his side. He agreed to report on the secret discussions in the king's council meetings as well as divulge all new and secret battle plans devised against the invaders.

Morlok made this offer in secret to Lucian only, knowing the noble could not resist the bait. In truth, Morlok intended to make Bordeaux his capital city as he rampaged through France to build his empire. The weak fool, Lucian, had no clue the only fate that awaited him was rotting in a dungeon beneath the throne Morlok would claim.

With all the pieces in place, Morlok set his plan into motion. His spies drew maps from memory of seldom used roads so the rebel armies could move about in secret. He then sent men to spread discord among the people of Aquitaine with the purpose of convincing the commoners to welcome his invading army. Seeing that all was ready, Morlok divided his army into smaller companies. They would attack up and down Aquitaine's border, looking for weaknesses, making his army appear three times its actual size. Finally, once out in the open with King Jacques' forces fully committed, Morlok would quickly destroy the king's army because of Lucian's betrayal.

Sitting back in his camp chair, Morlok said, "I can already taste victory!"

Morlok's plan did not completely fall into place as the people of Aquitaine never rallied to his armies. Still, the other elements worked as planned. Reports reached the king of a terrible enemy attacking at various points on their border. There seemed to be no visible pattern of these random attacks. There was no goal other than to destroy and loot. King Jacques knew from experience that this was the Ignominia.

"So, Morlok finally came out of his hole," he said to Queen Amanda and Chancellor Gregory. "He can't possibly be thinking of attacking Aquitaine again. With the Houses united, our army is double the size we were the last time we met. Still, we must meet these attacks head on and quash his rebellion once and for all."

The queen was quiet, both the king and chancellor knew from experience she was uncomfortable with violence, uneasy about fighting being the first solution to any problem. However, with this enemy, Amanda admitted she could not find another solution.

Finally, she said, "Morlok is many things, but he is no fool. He is the personification of the dishonorable name he has given his army. Jacques, you shared with me the tactics he used and the ruthlessness he showed to his men and ours, but even then, there was always a purpose to his actions. If he is attacking, it means that he is confident of victory. It means he wants you to engage his army"

Gregory asked, "So you sense he has an advantage?"

"Yes! However, I fear we will not discover it until the war is upon us, and then it might be too late."

As the Ignominia's attacks increased along the frontier, they succeeded in confabulating Jacques and the Aquitaine commanders. It was clear that Amanda was correct in believing that Morlok had a well-thought out plan, but it was impossible to comprehend. Fighting Morlok's armies was like trying to catch smoke with his hands. They were always on the move and attacked where the commanders least expected it. The Ignominia always seemed to be one step ahead of them, and the people of the border villages started to flock towards Bordeaux with tales of a murderous army in black armor, led by ruthless leader.

Morlok sat in his camp and laughed. "The boy King will never know what hit him."

Chapter Twenty

The War Council

O ver the following weeks and months, the Ignominia Army was an elusive yet violent ghost, always one step ahead of the Aquitaine Army. Once the invading armies had marched to within sight of Bordeaux, King Jacques convened the final war council before fully committing Aquitaine's army to war. He gathered together the heads of the Noble Houses, Chancellor Gregory, Queen Amanda, and his commanders and advisors.

As they collected around a large table with a map of the area surrounding Bordeaux, the king said, "You are all aware of the situation. Small bands of Ignominia have been attacking at will and evading our soldiers. However, they have now assembled into a large army. We do not have firm estimates on the total number of men Morlok has, but our scouts believe it is at least equal to Aquitaine's." A shocked silence filled the room as he continued. "It is time to call our combined strength together and prepare for battle. Morlok is leading a ruthless army. However, I am confident that through working together, we will defeat them and rid ourselves of this scourge once and for all." As he looked around the table, he saw nods of agreement, except for the five members of the Steadfast.

"Pardon me, my king," Lucian said disdainfully, "it has become clear to us that your battle plans have been bungled from the beginning. Morlok has outfoxed you and outfought you at every turn. Why should we put our trust in your leadership?"

The room erupted with angry shouts and accusations flying across the table. After a time, there came a loud rapping sound that drew everyone's attention. The noise came from Chancellor Gregory's staff of office. He tapped it on the stone floor. "My lords, this is getting us nowhere. Yes, Morlok had the element of surprise and seemed to know our plans ahead of the battles. However, we now know where he is, and it is here," he said, pointing to the capital on the map with his staff. "Working together is the only way we can, as the king said, finally destroy the Ignominia."

A whispery laugh sounded across the table. "No, it is you who will be destroyed. We five Houses will not sacrifice our men or lands to this fight," Lucian said. With that, the Houses of the Bear, Fox, Panther, Eagle, and Mouflon left the council chambers. The king and queen looked at each other as they felt Morlok's trap snap shut.

Even though the king seethed with rage at this betrayal, he focused on the situation at hand. His army, now reduced to half of its fighting strength, was the only thing that stood between the capital and the Ignominia.

No, my husband, Amanda's voice said in his mind. *Remember our friends and allies of the forest. This is now their war, too.*

Closing his eyes, the king remembered the Guardian granting permission to the king and queen to address the Woodland Folk about the threat the Ignominia posed to the people of the stone city and forest alike. On the appointed day, Jacques and Amanda stood in the middle of the Guardian's Clearing, surrounded by representatives of all the different beings living in and around the forest. Jacques thought it best that Amanda spoke to them about the rampaging army approaching the city and the forest. She described the outrages the Ignominia had committed, including the clear cutting of whole forests and the wholesale slaughter of those living there. She told them of the great need Aquitaine had and asked for their help against this enemy.

The request was met with a silence that grew until finally, they felt more than heard the deep, powerful voice of the Guardian of the Forest. "You have spoken well and most respectfully, Queen Amanda. We have already heard from our distant brothers and sisters of these outrages you have described. However, we have not heard from the king. What would you have us do, King Jacques of Aquitaine?"

The king stood still and prayed for the right words. "Fellow citizens of this land, throughout the centuries, the lives of the humans and the Woodland Folk have often intersected, but seldom has mankind given you the respect deserving of those who inhabit this land with us." He heard murmurs of agreement and continued. "I understand your reluctance to become involved in this uniquely human and horrible endeavor. I will not minimize the danger to you. I have fought this enemy before. They are cruel and ruthless. The chances are many of you here today will not survive the battle. Still, I know that should we humans lose this war, many more of you will die even if you choose not to fight. It is not by your choice or mine that you have become part of this war. However, you will either be a participant or a casualty. There is nothing I can offer you except the undying thanks and respect of the king and queen of Aquitaine and our pledge that, should Aquitaine survive, we will work together with the Woodland Folk to rectify the wrongs we humans have brought against you."

The Guardian's voice once again flowed through them. "That was well said, King Jacques of Aquitaine. We will consider your plea and should we agree, you will see us if the battle turns against you. For now, you and the queen may leave."

A clear path among those gathered formed for them, and they walked to their horses.

As they rode back to the palace, Amanda felt Jacques's troubled state. She gently touched his arm, signaling to stop. Turning to him, she said, "Have faith, dearest. The decision our friends must make is monumental. They must talk amongst themselves, and they must all be heard. I believe they will not let us face this alone. They have never met a human like you before. You are honorable and trustworthy, and they feel a connection with you that is even deeper than mine. The Woodland Folk sense their fates are tied to yours." Jacques looked in her eyes for a long moment, and she felt his tension ease. Nodding his head once, he said, "We have a long ride ahead of us."

With his eyes still closed, Jacques searched his memory for further hints or clues as to what the Woodland Folk would decide. He well knew of the wrongs the forests and its citizens suffered by the inhabitants of Aquitaine, but he took heart in Amanda's counsel that the Woodland Folk sensed their reign to be more respectful. The only hope he could find was there. As the memory of the meeting faded from his mind, the king forced himself to rejoin the war council and noticed Amanda was speaking.

Wondering what he'd missed, Jacques brought his full attention back to council in time to hear the queen say, "… and this is the place where my guards and I will join the fight."

The king's head snapped around. "What was that?" he said.

All eyes turned to him as the queen said, "Were you not paying attention? We were talking about how best to place our men should the enemy be successful in breaking through our lines at certain points." Pointing to the map, she continued. "Here is where I intend to stand and fight."

Immediately, the image of Amanda fighting and being struck down on a lonely hilltop flashed through his mind. The king flinched away from that picture. He involuntarily said, "No!"

The queen looked at him in shock. "No? What do you mean, no? Our army's strength is half of what we expected. We need every trained person to fight, and I intend to do my part. Otherwise, why have I been training with you these past years if not to fight by your side?"

Suddenly, all he could see was a dying Amanda lying in the mud, and he said, "No, I will not allow it."

Recognizing the look on both the king and queen's faces, Gregory said, "Your Majesties, perhaps this discussion would be better concluded in private."

The king and queen retreated into an inner chamber so they might continue the argument out of sight and hearing of the council. Guards stood ready outside the closed door with their spears crossed. The council members paced around the table, talking urgently among themselves.

Chancellor Gregory said, "This is no time for an argument like this. Not on the eve of battle."

Jacques stalked to the window and stared out into the night. He felt his anger and frustration grow hot. *Why! Why was she so stubborn? He was only trying to protect her and the kingdom.* "Do you not see that if we are both cut down, Aquitaine will fall?" he asked her. With the image of her dying body fresh in his mind, he wheeled around, eyes dark and furious.

"Amanda! Weren't you listening? Five out of the ten Houses are sitting this battle out! We are facing an army that has twice as many men at arms as we do, and they will do anything, ANYTHING, commit any atrocity, and kill anyone in their path. Aquitaine and her wealth are what they are after, and they will stop at nothing to get it. They will fight to the last man to get what they want! If I fall, you are the sole Sovereign! It will be up to you to continue the fight and rule once we defeat the enemy. Do you understand?"

Then he raised himself to his full height and said, "As your King, I forbid you to go to battle with us! That is final!"

Suddenly, it felt like all the air was sucked out of the room. Jacques knew he had gone too far, but he would not back down. Amanda slowly turned to face him, her green eyes glowing like emeralds on fire.

"You?" she scoffed. "You presume to talk to me like some child? YOU dare to forbid ME? You forget yourself, sir! I am queen of noble birth and of a noble house, unlike an upstart like you!"

It took an effort for Jacques to not take a step back from the power in her eyes and voice. Her words stung his face as if slapped.

"It is time you remember your place, sir! I WILL be in battledress at dawn with OUR army! I WILL fight! That is the end of it!"

The queen turned on her heel and stalked out of the room. The counselors scurried out of her way, looking at the king as he rejoined them. His anger spent. Jacques hung his head and wondered, *Is that what she truly thinks of me? If so, what is it I am trying to save?*

The king in him realized these thoughts were nothing but a dangerous distraction. Still, the man in him was crushed. Jacques shook his head, clearing his mind and reconvening the war council to review the battle plans and contingencies for the next day

Chapter Twenty-One

Aquitaine Goes to War

The king remained consumed in doubt, and with a wounded pride he did not sleep that night. Staring out the window of the inner chamber as the deep shades of blue slowly gave way to the soft hues of pink, red, and orange of dawn, Jacques saw none of the beauty as he kept fighting the battle in his mind, looking for something he knew he and the war council had missed. It was right in front of him, but he couldn't see it. Soon he heard a soft knock on the door. His squire had come to dress him for battle.

Later, King Jacques strode out of the chamber room arrayed in full battle dress. Strong and supple chain mail underneath bright, polished armor. It was both lightweight and strong, made from his design. The crest of Aquitaine emblazoned on his breastplate and an ancient and scarred golden battle crown sat on his head over the chain mail hood. His squire hurried after his liege with the king's cloak and sword. As Jacques stood over the maps and battle plans one last time, the squire buckled his sword around his waist and attached his deep royal blue cloak to his armor. On the cloak, the coat of arms for both his and the queen's House were embroidered in silver thread. His House showed a lion rearing up, claws spread. Hers, an Osprey in flight, wings spread, talons out. He looked every bit the warrior king.

The sounds of men cursing and horses' hooves clattering on cobblestones interrupted his thoughts, with Jacques's attention brought back to the present, he told the squire to inform the queen it was time. Then, ignoring the scared look on his squire's face, he walked down the stairs to the great hall and out into the cool predawn morning. He stood for a moment looking up at the bright stars once more, then mounting his war horse, he trotted to his field headquarters, knowing he would not enter the city again until the war concluded.

When the king arrived, he saw Amanda was already there and in the full battle dress of a warrior queen.

She is magnificent! Beautiful and resolved yet terrible and fierce! I almost pity the enemy she will face. She wore the same armor design as his with the same crest. Her battle crown was newer and brighter and without a blemish. *Soon, her crown will look like mine.*

The only difference in dress was her cloak, which bore the color of her House and was the same green color as her eyes. On it, both coats of arms were embroidered just as the king's, only the Osprey was more prominent on the queen's cloak, causing Jacques to smile. Typical, he said to himself. Still, he admitted he was proud and honored to ride into battle with her. He knew of no one he trusted more or had greater courage than Queen Amanda. He only hoped that she saw the gap in the battle plans he did not. She had always been better at chess.

Amanda saw him frowning and deep in thought. She was still angry, but she felt a lump in her throat looking at him sitting regal and strong on his mount, just like the kings of old. *How could she have said those terrible things to him? I sounded just like those children who mocked him so long ago,* Amanda thought as she focused on her husband's face. *Jacques looks preoccupied and worried.* Her eyes now burned with unspent tears, and her face was red with embarrassment. *I must tell him how sorry I am and ask for his forgiveness. It is impossible to love a man more than I love him!*

She moved to ride over but heard the horns calling them to battle formation. As the king and queen rode side by side at the front of the armies, both were lost in their thoughts. Jacques hated riding into battle with last night's words still between them. He regretted forbidding her to fight. *Of course, she would fight! She was born to fight, especially if someone threated her family, friends, or subjects.* Looking over at Amanda again, Jacques felt his heart skip a beat in his chest.

As the knights found their positions, a light rain began to fall. They all looked up, knowing that ground would soon turn to mud, making marching and fighting difficult and deadly. As the ground would get churned up by both army's feet, it will slow the cavalry down. Still, they resolutely formed their lines, row after row of proud and brave men, ready to fight for their families, friends, lands, and each other. Their ground was high and overlooked the once tranquil green valley where the enemy gathered. They saw the valley and fields were now dotted with hastily built earthworks. They thanked the Maker their position was well chosen and cursed the enemy for spoiling the land. The men looked over the field of battle with a practiced eye, assessing weaknesses they could exploit once the battle began, knowing full well that once the first arrow flew, their plans would disappear like smoke.

At the appointed time, trumpets sounded with the heralds calling the commanders of both armies to the chosen meeting place so they might entreat with each other one last time to avoid bloodshed. The king and queen rode together to meet with Morlok, the commanding general of the Ignominia. Queen Amanda got her first look at Morlok and saw he was indeed a giant. His armor covered his chest only, leaving his massive arms bare and showing the scars from his many battles. He slowly rode forward on the massive black warhorse chosen for its ability to bear his weight.

Both the horse and master wore matching black armor with no adornment except for curved horns jutting out from the helmet. Morlok removed his helmet, shaking out his shaggy grey hair and letting all see his pockmarked face. He gave the king and queen a mocking bow and smiled, showing his yellowed and broken teeth.

Saying Morlok was ugly sounds more like a compliment than the truth. Jacques thought.

"So," Morlok began, "you choose to fight and die rather than accept me as your rightful king! You even brought your woman so I may see the prize that awaits me after I destroy you."

Both the king and queen roared with laughter. Morlok's face darkened as King Jacques said, "Obviously you do not know my queen. The only prize you will get from her will be her sword splitting your grotesque skull! Still, don't despair, Morlok. It can only improve the look of you."

Amanda smiled, but her green eyes flashed, causing Morlok and his mount to flinch. She was furious that this…creature thought her so weak and helpless as to claim *her*! She said with a sweet smile, "No doubt, my husband, it would be but a slight improvement! The only way to enhance such a grotesque visage is to remove it altogether."

"Enough!" Morlok roared. "You have sealed your doom! I will crush your army! I will drink my wine from your skull! I will tear down your city block by block until there is not one stone standing on another! I will..."

Quietly Jacques said, "*IF* you could do any of that, you would have done it already. Come, my queen, I am bored with this ridiculous banter. It is time for battle!"

"Yes, my Lord, he goes on and on," the queen answered. "Besides, he breathes out the foulest stench. It almost makes one lightheaded."

With that said, they turned and rode back to their army, leaving Morlok's curses fading into the distance.

Chapter Twenty-Two

The Battle for Aquitaine

The king and queen slowly rode back to their battle lines to show Morlok they did not fear him or his threats. Queen Amanda felt the excitement and the jitters of one who had never experienced battle before. King Jacques, knowing what to expect in the way of blood, gore, and death, prayed for his queen and his men.

The king looked over at his queen and said, "Dearest, please forgive me for forbidding you to fight. I should have known better."

Queen Amanda looked down to hide the tears in her eyes and said, "I forgave you last night, my love. It is you who must forgive me the hurt my words caused you. You are our king, and you are my king. No one is more worthy of being in your place."

He took her hand in its armored glove and kissed it. "My beloved, I forgave before the sun rose this morning. Now, let us end this rebellion once and for all!" Amanda watched as his face took on a different look of determination and fury. His eyes were so dark they were nearly black, and his mouth took on a savage smile. Had she not known him so well, the queen would have backed away.

"Yes, my king," taking courage from him, "let us make today ours!!"

As they took their places, King Jacques nodded to his general to give the order to attack. Trumpets sounded, and flags waved as flight after flight of arrows blackened the sky, dealing death to both armies. Soon, the infantry advanced, stepping over their dead and wounded comrades to take their revenge. The sound was deafening as the two armies clashed together. Sparks flew as swords rang against each other and clashed on shields. Spears were thrown and arrows shot from others with tall longbows and deadly aim tore through the thick leather jerkins that some men wore for armor. The men yelled out battle cries as they advanced, and men screamed in pain from their wounds. Soon, the blood mixed with the rain turning the mud into a thick, red slurry.

It went on like this for half the day. The Ignominia pressed in on the Aquitaine army, and the proud warriors of Aquitaine pushed them back again and again. Finally, the trumpets sounded on both sides, signaling a break in the battle allowing the healers to care for the wounded left on the field. King Jacques looked down at the numbers of his men returning to their lines.

Too many have fallen or are wounded, he thought, and looking over, he saw the same realization in his commander's eyes.

"Why are we leaving the field?" the Queen asked. "What is happening?"

The King answered, "The first day of battle is done. Both sides used this day to test each other's lines for strengths and weaknesses. It will be worse tomorrow." He turned his horse towards his tent. As he rode to the tent, King Jacques felt the full weight of the day's events. These were his men he used as pawns in a massive chess game. He wondered at the numbers of wounded and killed, hoping they were less than the estimates he heard. As the queen rode beside him, she sensed what he was feeling and one thing he would admit to no one. That this was HIS war, and HIS battle and every casualty was HIS responsibility, and she could not help him bear the weight of it.

That evening, the war council met in the king and queen's tent and reviewed the day's battle and looked for ways to adjust the overall strategy.

"Has there been any word from the Steadfast Houses?" the King asked.

"None, Sire," Gregory answered. "They seem to await the outcome of the battle to either join you at the last moment to ensure glory for themselves or to sue for peace should we fall."

The King nodded. Yes, that sounds like Lucian. It is fortunate we have allies unknown to Morlok, but are as yet not committed.

After the council left, only the king, the queen, and Chancellor Gregory sat in the tent, quietly talking.

"Amanda," said the king, "I think it is time to contact our friends, telling them that tomorrow and the next day will sorely test us. They should ready themselves if they agree to come to our aid."

The queen nodded half-heartedly and said, "I agree, but I hate to involve them in this. They have little to do with the affairs of men."

"That is true," the king said, "but they live in this place too, and if the Ignominia wins, the fate of their world will be tied to ours."

The queen nodded again, stood, and left the tent to send the message through one of the Guardian's bird emissaries.

The second day of battle was worse than the first. Both armies hammered away at each other, and several cavalry charges ripped through lines on both sides, quickly reforming behind them and ultimately accomplished nothing. The Ignominia armies pushed the Aquitaine line back, and the queen with her guards joined, in the fight. She felt and heard the arrows as they pinged off the armor. She was, once again, thankful for Jacques and Leonitus' training. Both sides used massive trebuchets to fling huge boulders deep into the opposing army. At one point, the king led one charge into the Ignominia's flanks, hacking at the soldiers to his left and right while feeling their blows glancing off his armor. However, the charge did little to change the course of the overall battle. Both armies were too evenly matched to gain an advantage. The king and the queen recognized the only way the Ignominia could win was through their sheer numbers of men.

They also knew a full half of the enemy army was still being held back in reserve far to the rear, resting before they faced an exhausted Aquitaine on the third day.

Later that evening, the king asked, "Our army is maybe at two-thirds strength. Gregory, where do the other Houses stand? Will they join the fight?"

Gregory slowly shook his head. "No, Sire, they would rather see you and the kingdom fall than support you. The Steadfast will now only join us if we turn the tide of battle."

Turning to Queen Amanda, the king asked, "Have we heard from the Woodland Folk yet?"

"Not yet," said the queen. "Have faith, beloved. Faith can move mountains." With that, she kissed his forehead and went to bed.

Unable to sleep, the king walked to the tents where the wounded were being treated, speaking with the healers about the condition of his men. They told him they had already taken a great number of the most seriously wounded to the city, and the healers had divided the remaining wounded into three categories. The first group of those with minor wounds had already rejoined their companies. Every one of them preferred to live or die next to their brothers in arms for what surely must be the final battle of this war. The second group, while wounded, could still fight in some capacity if needed. The last group was the most critically injured and would not survive if moved to the city. Most, if they lived, would never fight again.

The King asked, "How many men have you treated?"

The healers looked down and said, "By our count, nearly half of our forces. However, Sire, many of those who had injuries not overly serious are still willing and able to join the fight."

The King showed no emotion as he thanked them for their service to his men. Jacques looked over at the second group of men, seeing the eagerness in their eyes to rejoin the fight. He also saw how young they were, some hardly past their Name Day. He turned and reluctantly told the Healer to gather the least wounded of his charges and have them muster to the army's rear as reserves. Those standing closest heard the king's order and cheered in gratitude for allowing them to rejoin the fight. The king nodded, blinking back tears, then turned and walked back to his tent.

Meanwhile, in the Ignominia camp, Morlok was already celebrating his upcoming victory with his commanders. "Tomorrow, we will crush them. My estimates show they are one half to two-thirds fighting strength." Looking at one of his commanders, Morlok said, "Tonight, under cover of darkness, call up all the reserves and move them into position. Tomorrow, we attack in two waves. One-half of our forces will attack head on along their whole line. Once we fully engage their army, the reserves will surprise them and attack their flanks from the gap in the hills they have left unguarded. Tomorrow night, I will sleep in the king's bed!" He then took a small keg of wine and uncorking it, guzzled it, letting the wine spill down his beard and armor.

Deep in the ancient forest, Woodland Folk met one final time to decide whether to join in the human's battle. There had been much debate since the king and queen had asked for their help in fighting the Ignominia.

Some said, "Let the human's fall. They have never shown themselves to be loyal friends to us!"

Others said, "We should join with Aquitaine. Those humans are not perfect, but we have heard from our brothers and sisters. Their homes and lands were cut and burned with no regard to those who lived therein. The Ignominia are far worse and will destroy our homes as well."

Finally, the Guardian spoke. "As you know, I have little interest in the affairs of mortals who walk the earth. I am ancient beyond all reckoning and have seen all ages come and go. I have observed those who were noble and virtuous and others who have committed great evil. The decision before us is to determine whether we can trust the words of the young king and queen, and that decision must be unanimous. Time is growing short; let us vote again."

Chapter Twenty-Three

The Third Day

The dawn of the third day of battle was heartbreakingly beautiful. As the king and queen looked up, they saw the sky was a deep, cobalt blue and dotted with brilliant points of light hanging between heaven and earth. Off to the east, they saw the slightest hint of a red dawn's arrival.

No rain would interfere with the terrible business of this day, thought the king and knowing his thoughts, the queen squeezed his hand.

"Have faith in your strength and that of our friends, my love. Have faith and let us face this day with courage. Because, no matter the outcome, we will face it together!"

In the Ignominia camp, the men were already making their final preparations for battle. Men had sharpened their swords. Armorers hammered out the dents in armor. Healers carried on their grisly business. The cooks made a meager breakfast using the last of their provisions. They would either dine that night on fine Aquitaine food or starve in their defeat.

Morlok was so confident in his plans, he didn't bother with a final check with his commanders as to placing his armies. He didn't even look over the field of battle one last time. When they tried to report that no one had heard from the reserve units yet, he waved them off. Morlok was sure that no one would dare disobey one of his orders. Everyone knew that to disobey an order or fail him would lead to unimaginable consequences.

"One last thing," Morlok said. "The king and queen are to be taken alive at all costs. Only a king may take the life of a king, and I WILL have my prize!"

As the king and queen met with their war council for the final time to discuss different battle strategies, the commanders argued for an hour among themselves about the way to best situate their companies.

Finally, the king spoke in a low voice, "That's enough argument. We need to make our plan. Queen Amanda, you have been silent. What are your thoughts?"

The commanders fell silent and gave their complete attention to their queen. She had proven herself to have a cool head in battle and an uncanny ability to place men where they would do the most good. The queen's strategy had turned the tide of battle several times, earning the commander's respect.

"Sire, we cannot rely on the rebel Houses for help. We have received reports that they have arrayed themselves in a battle line to our rear in case our lines break and they overrun us. Situated where they are, they hope to turn the tide against the enemy and then decide among themselves who will sit on our throne. I have not heard from the Woodland Folk yet, but I am confident they will aid us. However, they will do it in their way and on their terms." Then Queen Amanda made her recommendations for placing their forces.

The king looked around the map table, "Are we agreed? Good! Today the rebellion ends!!"

At mid-morning, the armies were finally in place. Long lines of brave men in bright armor stood at the ready with a forest of spears and pikes at their sides. The cavalry was also ready to move with the horses stamping impatiently for the upcoming fight. King Jacques looked over at Queen Amanda, knowing she too would be fully committed to the fighting. In a moment, their lives together played out in front of his eyes; She was everything a wife and queen should be, and yet she was so much more. King Louis had spoken true. Jacques, his House, and the kingdom were blessed because of Queen Amanda.

Suddenly, a deafening war cry sounded as the Ignominia launched a surprise frontal attack all up and down Aquitaine's line. There was a fierce abandon in the enemy's attack that the king had only seen on the day his father died.

"This is the final attack," he yelled, spurring his horse forward. "Commit all forces to the battle!"

A tremendous yell sounded all along the line as a surge of movement pushed forward. To his right, he saw that Queen Amanda spurred her mount into battle with the same fierce grin the rest of his men had.

He heard her yell, "For Aquitaine! For the King!" and then she was gone.

He sent one last prayer that all the training given her would be enough. In the distance to the rear, he heard faint horns calling a charge, but imagined it to be an echo and then he joined the battle.

The Ignominia were relentless in their attack, moving up and down the Aquitaine line. They were no longer fighting to win. The Ignominia fought with hatred for their enemy. They wanted to crush this army who dared to stand between them and their final prize. They had been starved, beaten, and forced to fight for years. Now all their pain and suffering would be rewarded.

They were spurred on by their commanders who yelled, "That's right, crush them! Think of what awaits you behind those walls! Only death awaits you out here!"

The men of Aquitaine suddenly heard and saw the cavalry of four of the Steadfast Houses thunder past and engage the enemy's flank. Together, they fought bravely and were equally fierce in defense of their city. It was clear, however, that even with the other Houses joining the battle, their numbers were still dwindling. The commanders knew it was because of the wounded men who had rejoined their brothers. Their spirits were willing, but they could not withstand the ferocity of the final attack, and were slowly pushed back.

The king supported the lines where he could, using all his training and experience, riding with no regard to his safety to wherever he saw the danger of a potential break. The sight of him driving into the enemy's attack and the sound of his sword blows on the enemy rallied the men as they pushed the enemy back. Casualties were dreadful on both sides and getting worse by the hour. It seemed to Jacques that if something didn't happen soon to turn the tide of battle, no one would be left to fight on either side.

The king saw Queen Amanda on a hill, surrounded by her men, holding back the enemy's counterattack. She fought bravely, using her Manticore training, but they were still losing ground. He rode to her side, dismounted and joined her in the fight.

Side by side they fought, slowly regaining the lost ground when he heard someone bellowing "Jacques, I see you now. Come and face your doom!"

Turning, he saw Morlok forcing his way towards him, pointing his notched sword at him and yelling, "I killed your father, and now I will kill you!"

However, before he reached the king, the sounds of battle changed from shouts of impending victory to those of pure terror. Suddenly, the Ignominia were retreating in large numbers. Morlok stared in disbelief at his army. They were on the verge of victory! What was behind this treachery?

Morlok did not know the commander of his reserves had moved the army through the forest during the night, hoping it would provide better cover. It was the kind of moonless night that was perfectly dark, and the men used torches to follow the path. Slowly, imperceptibly, the Ignominia were led away from the battlefield and deeper into the forest by Fire Fairies pretending to be guide torches. When the commander had finally realized they were lost, he'd ordered the men to assemble in a large clearing. The men, happy for the rest, sat down and built fires to drive away the oppressive dark.

Over time, they felt a growing malice that caused them to keep looking over their shoulders. Then they noticed the forest had gone completely silent. Not even a breeze blew through the trees. Around that time, the Aquitaine sentries heard what sounded like a whirlwind deep in the forest, accompanied by faint cries of terror being strangled out. No one witnessed what happened to the lost Ignominia army that night. The only evidence of their passing was some pieces of armor and a few broken swords. Afterward, anyone who passed through that clearing left those things lay where they were to rot and rust as a warning to those who would incur the Guardian's wrath.

As Morlok turned his attention to the gap in the hills where his reserves should be attacking, he saw, instead, a vast army of the Woodland Folk pouring through and routing his army. The Unicorns led the charge, trampling men as they ran, spearing others, and flipping the bodies over their backs. As the Unicorns spread out over the field, they chased down the fleeing army, kicking out with their sharp hooves at the rebels who tried to fight back. Following the Unicorns was an army of tall and hairy men, who attacked the Ignominia with clubs the size of small trees, throwing the huge boulders left from the trebuchets, crushing large clusters of men. Their hooting and howling war cries were as terrifying as they were deafening.

The Grand Surpis, now enormous, rushed into battle, charging through the Ignominia's lines, tossing men aside like dolls and crushing others under their massive bulk. As the Grand Surpis rampaged through the fleeing army, a cloud of Ice Fairies hidden in the Surpis' fur, now swarmed the Ignominia. The Fairies flew into the fleeing enemy's armor, freezing the arm and leg joints, making them easy prey for the winged

Manticores swooping down from the sky and ripping men apart with their sharp claws and teeth. The Vignes traveled underground and appeared underneath the Ignominia, wrapping themselves around the legs and torsos of the fleeing army and crushing the men in their armor with the Vignes steely grip.

Towards the rear of the army, a sudden hurricane of dried leaves appeared in front of the fleeing Ignominia. The Feuilles Colorees wove a swirling wall of leaves so dense the rebels couldn't find a way through. Those who tried were found afterward with all the flesh sliced off their faces and arms, flayed by the edges of the leaves as they swirled around them. It was then that infantrymen of the four Steadfast Houses fully caught up with the battle slicing and driving into the routed Ignominia Army. Thus, the Ignominia were trapped between a hammer of a reinvigorated Aquitaine and an anvil of the Woodland Folk and utterly destroyed.

Morlok couldn't believe his eyes! What sorcery was this? Plants and animals were routing his mighty army? It must be the queen. He'd heard rumors of her being a gypsy or a witch. No matter, he would soon bend her to his will, just as he did every other creature. Turning his attention back to the king, Morlok charged in a fury. Distracted, the king turned just in time to deflect the terrible blows raining down on his shield. Only the Manticore training saved him just then. Seeing Morlok fight, emboldened his most loyal knights to renew their attack against the queen's company.

As they traded blows, Morlok mocked Jacques saying, "What makes you think you can be a king? You are weak! I will show these people how a strong king acts and rules." Jacques didn't waste his breath replying. Instead, he looked for openings to exploit, wishing to end this once and for all. He glanced over at where Amanda fought and saw she held her own, but just barely.

Seeing the king distracted, Morlok drove his massive shoulder into Jacques, causing the king to lose his balance and fall, hitting his head on a rock. Morlok lifted his sword and brought it down on Jacques' sword, breaking it. Seeing Jacques dazed and defenseless, Amanda ran to his aid, blocking Morlok's sword from a killing blow.

Morlok laughed. "No matter, he isn't going anywhere. So, the pretty queen wants to play with swords? Well then, let's play."

As Amanda stood over Jacques, lying semi-conscious in the mud, she slowly gave ground to Morlok's blows on her shield. Amanda knew it was only a matter of time before her strength gave out. She heard his jeers and his laughter.

"Remove my head? I will remove HIS head and have it mounted on the wall above our bed," Morlok taunted.

Finally, his sword shattered Queen Amanda's shield. He grabbed her by the throat and lifted her off the ground: "Time to go my pretty little prize."

The queen then used a modification to her armored gloves, designed for hand to hand fighting. Installed within her gauntlets, were spring-loaded, steel Osprey talons, sharp and deadly.

Lashing out, she raked at his face with her nails and growled, "I am Queen Amanda of Aquitaine! I am not a prize for the likes of a creature such as you. I will see you dead first!"

Then, fast as a Manticore, she pulled a knife from her belt and drove it into Morlok's arm up to the hilt, twisting the blade in the wound.

Morlok, further enraged by the long, deep gashes along his jaw and cheek, wiped the blood from his eyes and pulled her face close to his saying, "Then join your crushed husband. If I cannot have you, then no one will!" and squeezed her throat.

Just before she passed out, the queen croaked, "Then make it quick. I thought your breath was bad before. Up close, it's unbearable."

Morlok screamed in rage and yanked the knife from his arm, thrusting it into Queen Amada, driving the point into her side, and dropping her into the mud at his feet. He raised his sword to end her mocking voice. At that moment, Vignes sprung out of the ground like a green tornado twisting themselves around Morlok's legs, torso, and arms. He raged as he fought against the onslaught. His massive arms tore and ripped the vines apart, and Amanda could hear tiny cries of pain from the vines.

As Morlok tore at the vines, he did not see a fully conscious and enraged king running at him. Swinging his broken sword one last time, Jacques separated Morlok's head from his body. Without waiting for the head to hit the ground, he turned to Amanda and saw the premonition he'd had in the war council: Amanda, bleeding out in the mud. As he gently picked her up, Jacques looked at her face, smeared with blood and mud. Amanda looked at him and smiled saying, "See? I told you it would improve his look." Then she slumped in his arms.

In the distance, he saw four of the remaining Houses fully attacking the enemy and realized those were the horns he'd heard earlier. The king seeing the Ignominia routed and running from the field in utter panic after the death of their leader, called for his horse and rode at a full gallop for the city's gates carrying Amanda to the one person who could help her.

Tears streamed down Jake's face. "No!" he said, "that's not right. Amanda doesn't die!! I can't lose both…" Jake wiped the tears with his handkerchief. "I have to see! I need to know!" he said as he turned to the next chapter.

Chapter Twenty-Four

The Healers

*J*acques carried the queen past the gates of the city and to the Hall of the Healers. No one dared approach him to help. The look of rage, despair, and pain made even his bravest knights lower their eyes in respect for their king and their beloved queen.

Once inside the gate, the King dismounted and ran into the hall hoping Amanda still might be saved by Quintus, his oldest and most trusted Healer. As he entered the hall, he confronted a new horror — row upon row of cots filled with his men, bleeding from their wounds. At a glance, Jacques saw bodies pierced with arrows and broken spears. Men, young and old, groaned from the deep slashes their enemies' swords had inflicted, while others were missing arms and legs. Moans and screams filled the air with calls for loved ones that many would never see again. In and amidst this chaos, healers and their attendants rushed between the cots, ministering to the wounded to the best of their abilities. The king's eyes were drawn to the back of the room, where rows of slain men were respectfully arranged, patiently waiting to be taken to the Houses of the Ancestors to join their fathers and ancestors in death.

Jacques looked from his men to his queen, draped in his arms. So many...gone. He thought. This doesn't feel like a victory. As the queen stirred in his arms, he called out, "Quintus, I need you!"

The old healer appeared and hurried towards the king, stopping short at the look on Jacques's face. "Quintus. You've watched over us these many years. You are the greatest healer in all of Aquitaine. Our queen needs all of your skill!"

Quintus tenderly took the queen's limp body from Jacques's arms, now soaked with her blood. "She will have my best, Sire," Quintus said and carried her to the place of the most critically wounded. For a moment, Jacques stared after them, saying a silent prayer and calling down mercy and healing. He never felt more hopeless and exhausted, but he still had a duty to perform.

In the short walk from the door to the rows of wounded, Jacques went from being a grieving husband to the king. He slowly walked among the cots and knelt by his men, speaking softly with them, seeking to comfort and ease their pain as best he could, and thanking them for their fealty to Aquitaine. Jacques lent his courage to those who were near death and those who faced a long and painful recovery. Last, the king approached his honored dead. Jacques silently cried as he walked to each body, gently removing the blanket covering their faces.

He softly spoke to each one, in turn, calling them by name, thanking them for their service and sacrifice. Jacques told each man to rest easy and not worry about their families, promising they would lack for nothing. He assured the men their children would hear of their bravery and honor in defense of the kingdom. The king pledged to engrave every one of their names at the main gate of the city so that all who passed would remember and stand in awe that such men as these had lived.

In doing so, Jacques poured out his grief for his men and his queen. The wounded, seeing their king so cloaked in sorrow, grew quiet in respect. Even those most grievously injured, bit their blankets and broken arrow shafts to silence their pain, honoring the weight of the king's anguish.

Quintus stood quietly behind Jacques, watching him make his promises to the last man. As the king stood, the healer noticed how slowly Jacques rose from his knees. Quintus' practiced eyes saw the king's exhaustion and the minor wounds he would tend to later. Jacques slowly turned, his head down, and the healer cleared his throat. Quintus saw the streaks the tears left in the mud and blood on the king's face. He watched the King's look of sorrow turn to one of resolve, which encouraged him.

Jacques, closed the distance between them in one stride and commanded, "Tell me!"

Quintus said, "She lives, majesty! Her wounds, while serious, will heal. The armor blunted the knife point and damaged nothing vital. However, as you know, she has lost a lot of blood. The queen has a slight fever, which I will carefully watch. I have done all I can, for now, and time will tell. Still, I have hope for a full recovery. I had her moved to your bedchamber for her comfort."

Forgetting protocol, Jacques took the healer up in a massive bear hug, lifting him off his feet whispering "Bless you, Quintus! Bless you!"

Quintus gasped, "Majesty, majesty, you're crushing me!" Smiling for the first time in weeks, Jacques set him down, slapping the healers back, "She lives!"

Jacques slowly limped into their bedchamber and looked at Amanda laid in their bed as her nurse finished checking her bandages. Covered with soft, thick blankets, she looked so very small and frail, unlike the strong and vibrant woman he knew her to be. Jacques picked up Amanda's battle crown from the pillow it rested on. He ran his thumbnail across the scars from where the arrows had glanced off, and he took note of the deep grooves that told of a sword's bite. *Her crown now looks like mine.*

He walked over, examining her armor hanging on a stand with a soldier's eye. The damage was impressive, scratches, dents, deep gouges, and the thin slit from the knife Morlok had used, attested to the fact that Queen Amanda had been in in the thick of the battle several times. He touched the dried blood that splattered the armor and inspected her cloak, looking at the holes where arrows had passed through. There were slashes in the cloth from swords.

Truly, Amanda, you have earned the title of a Warrior Queen! he thought. The nurse moved silently around the room, wiping the queen's brow with a cool cloth and murmuring soft words of comfort.

She turned to Jacques, curtsied, and said, "Have faith, your majesty. She's a fighter and strong. You'll see, she'll be up and around before you know it!" He gave her a tired smile and nodded for her to go.

Over the next several days, the king never left the queen's side, waiting for her to wake up, trusting in his commanders to do what was necessary. As Quintus cared for the queen, he also tended to the king's wounds. Jacques talked to her for hours, telling her the latest news, and reminiscing about their life together. He read her favorite books to her and sang her favorite songs. He would say or do anything to hear her voice or see her smile again.

When his voice grew horse, birds would fly through the open window and alight on Amanda's pillow, singing or chirping the news of the forest to her, bringing a welcome, faint smile to her face. The king rarely ate or slept. The little sleep he got, was plagued with nightmares and terrors. As time went on, he could tell her fever grew much worse. Quintus' strongest medicines and potions were not helping her. Jacques held her hand, talked to her, called her name, he wet her lips with a damp cloth, and begged her to wake up, but nothing worked.

Despite Quintus' best efforts, his queen was dying before his eyes. She cried out with words that made no sense. She would sit up with bright, feverish eyes full of terror, silently begging for help he couldn't give her. He saw the effect the fever had on her body. Even unconscious, it contorted her with pain. The only relief she had was when the Guardian sang his song of healing to her through the window. Jacques walked to the bed and slowly knelt. His tears dropped on her hand as he held it in his large, callused one, and brought it to his cheek. He prayed for healing and ended the prayer with a whispered "Please."

Jacques lost all sense of time as he held the queen's hand. He looked long at the face he loved. The face he knew in all her joys and sorrows. As he brushed a strand of hair off her face, Jacques felt something break inside his chest. Suddenly all the pain and loss of his life came crashing out as if a dam had burst. He thought of his years of alienation, his mother and father: gone. Jacques remembered the men lost and wounded during the battles of the rebellion fought with the Ignominia. Now as king, the last battle… his battle, the rows of cots of wounded and dying. The rows of both young and old who would not live to see another sunrise and those who had already passed to what was beyond…and now her!

Amanda had never asked for any of this, not to be queen, not to rule. This was all his decision. All she ever did was love and trust him and fight fiercely at his side for those she loved and cared for, not once giving a thought to her own safety. She gave everything she was to others and left nothing for herself. How could he bear to lose the one who meant the most to him?

Tears filled his eyes while he softly spoke to her. "Amanda, my beloved, there are some things you need to know." Jacques hung his head as words came tumbling out from his heart. "My love, I have never been good at sharing my feelings, even with you. Somehow you always knew what I felt without me saying a word. Still, I have to say this. You need to hear me say, since the day we met, you have been a wellspring of joy, filling my life. Amanda, you and your love are what I treasure most in this life. All that I am, all that I have accomplished, is because of your unwavering belief, faith, and confidence in me."

He took a deep breath and began again. "It was you who taught me how to trust because you have shown me loyalty beyond question, and only you know all my fears, thoughts, and doubts. Amanda, I am king, but you are my equal in every way. You are unmatched in courage, intelligence, and compassion. From you, I have learned to live my life to the fullest, seeing every day as a precious gift, and freely forgiving the wrongs of the past. You taught me to dance to the music in my head and how to laugh out loud again. Amanda, you saw me when no one else would, giving me the courage to break from the shell I built around myself. It was only when you showed me love that I realized how lonely my life had been before you. Phillip was right when he said it was impossible to know what love is without knowing what love is not. I see now that, except for my parents, all I've known is what love was not. It was you who showed me what true love is."

"Have I ever told you that King Louis once said both the kingdom and I would be blessed because of you? He was right! I have been blessed beyond measure by your love, and by a life I never imagined possible. Amanda, there is one thing I know to be true. I am convinced that in every way possible and even in ways that are not, you saved me. You saved me from an empty life. You saved me from a life of oblivion. You took my hand and called me out of my loneliness. Please, please, come back to me, love. Don't go anywhere without me." Tears streamed down Jacques's face as he lay down beside her, and taking his Amanda in his arms, he fell into a deep and exhausted sleep.

Light streaming through the window awoke Jacques later the next day. Amanda was curled up under his arm with her arm draped across his chest.

As he stretched, he heard, "It's about time you woke up, sleepyhead."

He was about to glare at the nurse when he realized it wasn't her voice. He turned his head to see Amanda smiling up at him.

She gently touched his face and said, "Jacques, I was lost in the darkness, but I knew you were always at my side. Your voice and your faith led me back to the light and to you. I heard all the wonderful things you said, and yes, I knew how you felt all along, but thank you for saying them. It has been my joy to give everything I have and all that I am to you. Jacques, you too have given me a life and a love I never imagined possible, and you have unconditionally accepted me for who I am. For all I am to you, you are all of that to me. Though my love, you were only half right. We saved each other."

Chapter Twenty-Five

Reckonings

Immediately after the battle and for some days afterward, men moved about the battlefield. The men carried the wounded to the Healers and recovered the honored dead. It was a gruesome task carried out by men privileged to care for their fallen brothers. An Honor Guard was formed to recover the remains of the many magical creatures who heroically gave their lives to save Aquitaine and the Forest. The Woodland Folk were carried with great care to the edge of the forest and laid in an open field.

That evening, guards were posted to safeguard the remains and were faced away from the forest as a sign of respect. As dawn's first light reached the field, the men, discovered all the bodies were collected sometime in the night. They never heard a thing. Ever since that day, wildflowers of a kind no one had ever seen before, and in every imaginable shade and color, blanketed the field, even in winter. The next year, the Guardian caused seven saplings to sprout in the field, and they grew into enormous trees to honor each kind of Woodland Folk who sacrificed themselves for the forest. Later, the queen made a royal proclamation naming the field The Guardian's Garden and forbidding anyone from entering the field or picking the flowers.

There was no grand parade or banquet held after the Battle of Aquitaine. There was too much to do and far too much sorrow. Over the next days and weeks, families gathered to commit their departed loved ones to the care of their ancestors. The king made sure he was present at every ceremony to reaffirm his promise and give his thanks and respect.

Once all the dead were laid to rest, and the queen was again strong enough to resume most of her duties, she joined the king in the throne room to sit in judgment of the Steadfast Nobles. As a graphic reminder to everyone assembled as to why they were gathered, the king and queen dressed in their battle armor chest plates, still splattered with blood and scarred from the damage of the fight. The queen's armor showed the hole where Morlok drove a blade into her side. On their heads were placed scarred and battered battle crowns.

As the audience gathered, all commented that the stern looks on the king and queen's faces were terrible to behold. Most expected no mercy as the king called the Heads of the Bear, Fox, Panther, and Mouflon Houses before them.

He said, "Is it true that on the third day you finally joined with us in the fight?"

"Yes, your Majesty" they answered.

The king and queen were silent for a long time, making them feel the weight of their stares. The king asked, "Why?" As each lord answered, they said, after the battle on the second day, Lucian let slip about his agreement with Morlok and how he gave the enemy all of Aquitaine's secret plans. Lucian bragged that after the battle, he would be crowned and claim the queen as his consort.

Each lord told of his horror when he recognized Lucian's influence and betrayal. Once the lords realized how they were manipulated into joining the wrong side of the war, they met in secret, deciding to break with Lucian and join the king's side. Each lord explained they attacked in surprise to send Morlok's army into disarray.

The king looked over to his commanders who reluctantly nodded their heads in agreement to the strategy. Looking over at the queen, he asked, "Queen Amanda, do they speak the truth?"

After a moment of reflection, she answered, "Yes, Sire, these lords were taken advantage by Lucian's duplicitous nature. While not blameless, they recognized their error and rectified their actions. I will leave it to you alone to determine their fate."

The king sat completely still, staring at the lords as they stood before him.

Finally, he said, "I agree, my queen. Their weak minds were betrayed, not Aquitaine. My lords, your sentence is this. You will take your companies to the field to track down and destroy the remaining, fleeing enemy. You will accomplish this at your own expense, and you will take as long as needed to complete this task. Once I am satisfied you were successful, you will swear allegiance to BOTH the king and queen of Aquitaine, and then you may return to your lands with your honor fully restored. After that, you will select a portion of your most suitable men, whose sole duty will be to work with the Woodland Folk to repair and restore Ancient Forest from the centuries of human damage. These 'Rangers' will then continue to serve and protect the forest from any human who would hunt, gather, deface, or encroach on their borders."

The Lords fell to their knees, saying, "Thank you, thank you, my king and queen."

After the lords filed out of the room, the king told his Lord Chancellor, "Bring us, the traitor Lucian."

Lucian entered the room trying to look contrite and sorry, but that mask soon fell away, replaced by a look of angry arrogance.

Chancellor Gregory said, "Lucian, you are charged with the crimes of High Treason and Conspiracy and…" It took Gregory the better part of an hour to finish the list.

"Lucian, you have not failed to live up to our lowest expectations of you," said the king. "Do you or anyone else have anything to say in your defense?"

Lucian looked around the room with what seemed like pleading eyes, even managing a tear or two. When no one came to his aid, he looked at the queen saying, "Please, my queen, I was only trying to help."

Queen Amanda lifted her hand, stopping him, and in a voice devoid of emotion said, "I am not YOUR queen. You never swore allegiance to me!"

"My apologies, your majesty," Lucian sniveled. "Still, you heard how the king wouldn't listen to my counsel. I had nowhere to turn, so I looked to my fellow nobles who talked me into leading them. I didn't want to do it. I wanted to stay faithful to the crown, but…" Much to everyone's regret, he whined on like this for some time, pleading for sympathy, and found none.

After Lucian finally ran out of words, the chancellor said, "Lord Lucian of House Eagle, you have been found guilty of High Treason, Conspiracy, and a host of other crimes against Aquitaine. The king will pronounce your sentence."

The king and queen looked at each other for a long time, mentally debating with each other about the sentence. Finally, the king said, "Lucian that was quite a performance. By the laws of the land, I should hand you over to the executioner right now."

Lucian looked back at the king with hatred in his eyes and started towards the throne, but stopped after seeing the king's stare. "Lucian, you are a coward and the worst kind of man. You are a predator. You take advantage of people's better natures and use them for your own purposes. You have no place in this kingdom. However, even though you have betrayed her at every opportunity, you have the queen to thank for your life. She has urged me to consider forgiveness, even in your case. Although I am not quite sure if this is what she had in mind."

Glancing at Queen Amanda, the king saw she had a slightly bemused smile. "I judge that, for the rest of your life, you will be chained by the ankle to your commanders, and together, you will rebuild all of what your friends burned and destroyed. When you have finished with that, you will, for the rest of your natural life, build roads, schools, clear fields, and any other act of public service we think would benefit the people of Aquitaine. Your fortune will be forfeit and given to the wounded, the widows, and children of our fallen warriors."

"How do you wish to express your thanks for the queen's mercy?" Gregory said.

Lucian then spit on the floor.

"Charming," said the queen. "Take him away to begin his sentence."

However, before Lucian turned to go, Chancellor Gregory said, "Sires, what should we do with the traitor's lands?"

The king thought a moment, and asked, "His lands border upon the Ancient Forest as well as those adjoining it?"

"Yes, Sire."

Then looking over at Queen Amanda he said, "If the queen agrees, we proclaim those lands to be ceded over to the crown and awarded to the Woodland Folk to govern as they will, with our eternal thanks for coming to our aid when all seemed lost."

After hearing this, Lucian raged and fought against his guards as they dragged him from the room. The next day, a royal proclamation was sealed in a golden box to keep it safe. The king and queen personally delivered it to the Guardian of the Forest, and the king read a copy of the proclamation aloud to the host of Woodland Folk. Then the queen told them about the rangers and how they would work together at the Woodland Folk's direction to restore and protect the forest. The Guardian, with great solemnity, officially declared the woods would now and forever be known as the Forest

Kingdom, and it still known by that name to this day by that, although none but the Woodland Folk remember why.

CHAPTER TWENTY-SIX

Present Day

Jake pressed his head back into the chair's thick cushion, closed his eyes, and smiled. He remembered the days after the Ignominia's final defeat. Aquitaine, finally safe from outside threats, could focus on building the new future that King Louis predicted. The fields of war were reclaimed, and the scars on the landscape were healed. It was a metaphor for what was to happen as King Jacques and Queen Amanda's reign ushered in a new renaissance for every person in Aquitaine.

Schools were built and staffed by the best instructors available, attended by both boys and girls from the kingdom's cities and villages. Literacy improved, and with access to new information, life improved for the subjects of Aquitaine and surrounding provinces. The king and queen made it a policy to freely share any new theories or improved methods developed by the scholars and citizens of Aquitaine. Initially, this practice was viewed by other courts with suspicion and skepticism. However, when Aquitaine showed herself to be true to her word, scholars from all over Europe flocked to Bordeaux to study and take part in the open and intellectually free atmosphere found in the new schools and universities of Aquitaine.

Even Chancellor Gregory was surprised by the effect this one, simple action brought to the kingdom. Farmers prospered by using new techniques in planting and caring for their crops. The Arts and Humanities flourished with troupes of actors and troubadours traveling about the cities, towns, and villages bringing with them music and plays and dramatic readings from authors across Europe and beyond. Schools of art and sculpture grew up around Bordeaux. Under the reign of King Jacques and

Queen Amanda, life improved not only for the people of Aquitaine but for those of the surrounding regions and kingdoms, ushering in a time of peace for many years to come.

After much time and hard work, the Forest Kingdom was restored to its ancient state. The rangers and Woodland Folk worked together to mend the scars made by the humans over the generations. The Woodland Folk showed the men where the various saplings and plants grew ready to be transplanted and replanted, restoring not only the environment but the beauty of the forest. When time allowed, Jacques and Amanda walked and rode through the Forest Kingdom, greeting their old friends and meeting new ones. Jacques would sometimes visit the Guardian, and they would have long talks together about things that only they knew. Amanda would visit new families and sit and play with the chicks, kits, pups, and saplings of her many friends. Often, the king and queen would ride into the forest, heads bowed with the weight of their office and ride out days later, dirty and disheveled but laughing and singing to each other.

Jake's heart swelled when he thought of the beautiful children of the king and queen, Prince Leo and Princess Rachel. Born three years apart, they grew straight and tall and increasing in intelligence, quick wit, and the abilities of their mother along with the insatiable curiosity of their father. As Leo and Rachel grew, they were exposed to a life of service to others and developed a love of learning and reading. The prince and the princess also came to know, love, and respect the Forest Kingdom and all the Woodland Folk. Soon after the children were born, they were introduced to the Guardian and a gathering of the forest citizens and spent many happy days running and playing with their forest friends. Jacques and Amanda grew to love their children more with each passing year, and the years were passing.

Jake recalled how age came upon them slowly. Jacques and Amanda were still active into their later years exploring the forests of Aquitaine, practicing the Manticore martial arts, and playing with their children and those in Bordeaux. They kept their minds sharp by reading, sharing and sometimes debating their thoughts with one another, as they faced the challenges of ruling Aquitaine.

However, even the most active eventually slows down, and Jacques felt his age more than Amanda. One couldn't tell his age by his face as much as how his hair was almost completely white. The dark streaks of hair became fewer as the years passed. Because of the injuries he sustained in the many battles he'd fought, he often ached in the damp evenings or limped slightly as he walked across the room. There came a time when even riding his horse, Charger, the animal he loved the most, became too painful. However, it didn't stop Jacques from visiting his old friend to scratch his jaw, recall their glory days, and feed him apples and carrots. Whenever the king approached the stable, Charger would snort and stamp his feet to show he was ready for the saddle and a good gallop. However, neither rider nor horse was in any condition for a gallop.

Amanda aged, but except for an occasional twinge in her back, she was still as active as ever. As the years passed, she only grew more beautiful. Amanda allowed her hair to grow longer, and it slowly showed streaks of grey that only highlighted her loveliness. The people would often see her quickly walking through the streets of the city. Often, Amanda was approached by someone who needed to talk with her, or she would stop to say hello to people who she knew were too shy to come to her.

She never lost her ability or habit to say hello to the different animals who crossed her path. Many times, the queen would sit on a hay bale and let kittens roll around on her lap, playing with the ribbons from her dress. Sometimes one kitten would get offended by something she said in jest, and Amanda would always sincerely apologize. Everyone realized Queen Amanda was the blessing that King Louis foretold so many years ago and the king and queen were more deeply in love than ever.

Jake picked up the book and turned to the final chapter.

Chapter Twenty-Seven

Goodbyes

*N*ot long after Jacques 80th birthday celebration, he began to walk noticeably slower. His limp was more pronounced, and his breath shorter. When Amanda showed concern, he waved it off and make some joke about it. However, both Jacques and Amanda knew his time was getting shorter. He was more grateful than ever that years before, he and Amanda had abdicated the throne to their son Leo and remained as his advisors until he was fully ready to reign himself.

Now, with Leo married to his queen, and with Jacques and Amanda's daughter Rachel married and crowned as queen in a nearby kingdom, Amanda and Jacques felt life had finally settled down for them to spend time as they wished. They made plans to travel to see all the places they'd read about. They still danced at a moment's notice, sometimes on the street, laughing until they cried. The couple still talk late into the night and argue points about which they felt most passionate. Last, they spent time with the Woodland Folk every chance they could.

Then, one morning, Jacques found it hard to get out of bed, even with Amanda's and his squire's help. Amanda called for the Healers, but there was nothing to be done. The former king was slowly dying before their eyes. Jacques spent time with Leo, telling him how much he loved him and how very proud he was to have him for a son. Jacques dictated a letter to Rachel, telling her the same and how honored he was to be her father. Every night, Amanda would lie in bed with him, holding him and running her fingers through his long hair. They would quietly talk of their life together, and she laughed at his silly jokes, even as tears filled her eyes. While Jacques slept, Amanda would sing his favorite songs to him. Sometimes she whispered in his ear how much she loved him and how adored she felt by him. Amanda told him how proud she was to be his wife and how she would do it all over again.

Finally, late one day, as the sun's last warm rays bathed his face, Jacques looked into Amanda's eyes and said, "Beloved, I will soon join my fathers. I want you to know how much I have cherished every moment with you. You have been my joy and delight. Without you, I would have only been half the man I grew to be. I have loved no one as truly and completely as I have you. Don't cry for me, dearest. Our story doesn't end here. I will wait for you on the other side to greet you into our eternity." With unbidden tears streaming down her face, Amanda held him closer, took his hand, and bent down to receive his final kiss on this earth.

Jake closed the book with his hand still between the pages. *That is a fitting end to such a wonderful life. To be held close by the one you have spent a lifetime loving and growing old with.*

He thought about Manda, his children, and his granddaughter. He marveled at how blessed he was to have had such a wonderful family. He thought of all the things he had done in his life with them, his writing, the adventures he had in the real world, his friends, and his books. He had no regrets, knowing he had lived a full life filled with wonder made more so by his curiosity and imagination. Last, he thought of his queen, knowing Amandine was Amanda, who had become real for him, and he became Jacques for her. He smiled as he remembered their first disastrous meeting. He thought of his becoming King Jacques of Aquitaine and of how he ruled the kingdom with Queen Amanda as equals. Jake marveled at the adventures they had in exploring the forests and lands of their kingdom. He thought of the strange and wonderful beings they met along the way. He remembered the battles they fought together and how Queen Amanda fought as fiercely as his best knights. She truly was a warrior queen.

Jake thought back on his last tour of the castle in Bordeaux, culminating in a walk through the royal crypts. The sound of his footsteps and click of his cane had echoed on the ancient flagstones as he had slowly strolled past the elaborate sarcophaguses holding the remains of the kings and queens of Aquitaine. Finally, Jake came to the one he was looking for and looked at the sculpted image carved on the lid. His eyes had filled with tears as he'd looked upon the face, her beautiful face, forever frozen in marble. As Jake blinked away the tears, his eyes drifted down to the bronze plaque, secured to the marble. His fingers traced the words as he read:

Amanda of Aquitaine

Queen

Wife

Warrior

Mother

Healer

Teacher

Advisor

"...blessed to be a blessing."

Last, of all, he remembered the words Lord Phillip said so long ago. "How can you know what love is, without knowing what it is not?"

Thank you, Amanda and Amandine, because of you, I know what love is.

Jake's family and his personal physician interrupted his thoughts as they entered the room. He knew his time was near, and he wanted to say goodbye to his family. He looked at his children Gerard and Amélie, telling them how much he loved them and how proud he was to be their father. He then turned his attention to his only grandchild, Frances.

He smiled saying, "Oh Franci, don't be sad. I'm only saying goodbye for a little while. We will see each other again when you get to be my age. However, before I go, I would like you to have this book. It is the most wonderful and curious book I've ever owned. Read it and make its adventures your own. I want you to remember one thing my uncle told me long ago. If you truly love a character in this book, they will love you back, and the story will become real to you. Franci, you don't understand that yet, but you will."

He smiled and closed his eyes, feeling arms cradling him and recognizing the scent of Manda's favorite perfume. *Manda, my love.*

Jake felt the gentle kiss of her lips on his and heard her voice say, *It is time, mon amour. It is time to come home and be with me forever.*

"Finally," he whispered as a single tear rolled down the side of his face and with a gentle smile, Jake drifted away for the last time.

Franci buried her face in Jake's chest and sobbed until she felt her dad's hand on her shoulder and knew it was time to go. She gently took hold of the book and slowly pulled it, but it felt like grandpa's hand was being held. As it slowly and reluctantly came free, Frances could have sworn she heard a soft sigh from the book.

On the way home, she traced the gold-embossed title with her finger, The Girl Who Explored the World. Opening the book to the first chapter she read:

Chapter One
Signorina Francesca

There once was a young woman named Francesca who lived long ago in the faraway Republic of Venice…

The End

ABOUT THE AUTHOR

Writer. Storyteller. Travel Junkie. Activist. Businessman. James Pindras was that kid in sixth grade who stared out the window at imagined pirate ship battles rather than listening in class. James draws upon his many experiences as well as his active imagination in weaving his tales. He has served in the non-profit world for over twenty-five years. Originally from the Chicago-area, James now lives in Alabama. He is a Concordia Publishing House contributing author.

Facebook: jpindras author

Instagram: @jpindrasauthor

Web :jpindrasauthor.com